The Logician

Taylor!
From "Aunt" Cheryl

Dedicated to all the hard-working
Classical Conversations Challenge students and especially the
beloved ones that I have had the privilege of tutoring!
Mrs. K

CONTENTS

Prologue

Wendel, before he was known as Dr. Salomon, took a trip. He needed rest. Not yet in his mid-twenties, he was tired and weary of his many years of collegiate discoveries at the great institution of learning, Oxford University.

Imagining the most isolated place he could escape to and always being a bit curious, he chose Siberia.

Wendel packed a bag, bought a train ticket, and spent the hours staring out the glass window, watching blindly as trees, rivers, and meadows flew by.

He felt empty and numb but did not wish for a single thought to cross his mind that would cheer him up. As the miles passed, he woodenly went through the motions of staring and eating and sleeping, then to staring again.

On the third day of this, the intelligent young man sensed an understanding to his despair that crept into his consciousness. It was loneliness.

A week later, Wendell exited the station in Tartu, Estonia and asked for directions to an inn where he could stay the night. He was directed toward the center of town. He walked slowly dragging his suitcase behind him until he came upon a simple, ancient, brick building.

He felt a great peace wash over him as he entered through the arched doorway. He credited it to the clean, empty, rustic surroundings of the main room. It was an uncluttered space that gave his mind no distraction.

Several wooden tables were prepared for guests, and he sat at the one nearest the door. There was a girl about his age with hair pulled back into a loose braid serving the guests.

He ordered his dinner as she swept by his table, and she soon brought boiled potatoes and sausages. Somehow, he felt comforted, for that is what a smile and delicious food can do. He called to the young lady serving the meals. Guessing her to be a simple, hard-working girl yet unknowledgeable of English, he wanted to communicate a few words of thanks.

"Ah, what is your name, dear lady?" He asked loudly and slowly. "I want to thank you for the smile and the good meal?"

"Ruth," she replied.

"That is a noble name that appears near the beginning of the Bible, she was a loyal person if I remember correctly," he proudly recalled after realizing she was proficient in the English language.

"And, in the lineage of Jesus!" she added.
Wendell lifted his eyebrows, "I did not know that."

"Oh, yes, her son was King David's great grandfather."

Wendel was taken aback as she had taught him something that, in his many years of study, he had not learned.

"Of course," he thought to himself, "I can't possibly know everything."

"May I ask you a question, Ruth?"

"Yes," she answered.

"What do you think is the most important thing in the whole world?" Philosophy was creeping back into his troubled thoughts.
"That is easy, virtuti et veritatis," she smiled and turned to go.

"Wait, one more question!"

"Yes?"

"Will you marry me?"

"What! I don't even know your name!"

Wendel did not make it to Siberia. It would have to wait for another time. He stayed in the beautiful town of Tartu for several months and won over Ruth's father, mother, sister, brother and finally, at last, Ruth herself!

Twenty-five years later, Ruth grabbed Wendel's arm in the middle of the night.

"What is it, my dear?"

"Shh, Wendel, someone is under the bed, it is shaking!" So was Ruth's voice.

Wendel agreed, "So it is, but I can prove that no one is under the bed." He switched on the small lamp on the table next to him, pushed himself sideways and upside down and peeked under the bedspread.

"See, no one could get underneath, and if they did, why would they shake? If they had convulsed, even that would not shake the entire bed."

Her grip relaxed, "Well, then, what is it!"

"Didn't you ever have earthquakes in Estonia, my dear?"

CHAPTER 1

Doctor Logic and Son

Occasionally Scotland Yard, when they were particularly baffled, would call upon Sir Wendel Salomon. Professor Salomon, called Dr. Logic behind his back by his students, was short, slim, and graying. He touted a stylish goatee and always (whether it was winter, spring, or fall) wore a scarf around his neck to ward off the English dampness. He was not only knighted, but also highly honored among rank and file. He was a man of morals and principles. Under his most illustrious wing was his son, Winston, whom he endeavored to instill these same character qualities and the ability to deduce and logically solve the dilemmas of life.

"Let's go, my boy," directed Sir Wendel to his son while replacing the phone receiver. A call had come in requesting his deductive reasoning skills. Winston bounded behind, grabbing a jacket as he ran. He knew that if he couldn't keep up, he would be left behind. A quick note was left on the table for Mrs. Ruth Salomon, who was the organist at choir practice that evening.

The detecting team's destiny was none other than the massive halls of higher learning itself, Oxford University, the very halls in which Sir Wendel glided through in robes and regalia when he chose to teach a term. His current interests warranted a sabbatical. He had hopes of answering questions concerning curious matters, which would eventually take him to foreign lands.

The father-son team followed the chief inspector and his team into the halls of science to a room marked "Entomology." Professor Hardcastle was lying on the carpet, still and stiff. His dull eyes were wide-open, gray hair wild and one index finger pointed. Sir Wendel took it all in. Sixteen-year-old Winston, not the queasy type, yet not altogether thrilled with looking death in the face, stayed close behind his father. Chief Inspector Newbury was trying to hide his irritation at having a kid in the room, but he knew that he would have to keep it to himself. Winston, being bright and deductive himself, noticed everything: the tautness of the body, the shocked look on the face of the corpse, the overturned coffee cup, and the open thermos on top of the desk.

"Why is he pointing at the thermos?" thought Winston.

"Best check the thermos for poison," mumbled the inspector as he handed the protective gloves to Sir Wendel and Winston. He then slipped on a pair himself.

"On it, Chief," replied the sergeant. As the sun was setting further down the horizon, the reading light on the dead man's desk was shedding little light on the matter. The dark corners of the massive and musty room seemed to be closing in on the inspection.

"Can't we get more light in here?!" the sergeant insisted. Finally, after a light switch was found, the room was transformed to near daylight and with it came a few gasps—one being Winston's.

The high ceilings and dark wood-covered office lit up to reveal jars of a variety of invertebrates. The "bug professor" was a collector and hoarder of insects which spilled over into other lovely specimens: lizards, crawfish, snakes, all sizes and shapes of arachnids, all pickled in formaldehyde and carefully labeled.

Winston's thoughts were on future nightmares, the inspector's thoughts were on the irritation of odd cases. The quiet Dr. Salomon was staring closely at the desktop and even closer at the pointing index finger while using a large magnifying glass. He requested an evidence bag, which was quickly produced. After a careful tweezing, he dropped something miniscule into the receptacle.

The coroner was called in and had the body removed. Dr. Salomon gathered up the papers that were strewn across the deceased man's desk. He thumbed through a daily planner, a large notebook listing the collected specimens, and another notebook with the handwritten title, *Other Rare Species*. He became aware of a noise just above him on a shelf. Dr. Salomon froze, dropping the books and papers. He spoke sternly with the kind of emphasized monotone voice that only parents seem to possess.

"Winston, I need you to leave this room now." Winston, recognizing the tone of his father's voice, backed out of the room, as icy fingers of fear seemed to close around him. A chirping and high-pitched warble echoed throughout the rooms.

Winston wondered, "Why, it's just a bird. What's the big deal?" The inspector, minutes earlier, had already ushered his team out of the room. He was more than ready to close shop. His stomach growled, his head hurt, and he was exhausted. His phone rang.

"What!" loudly barked the man.

"I am sorry, Inspector, but we have a serious problem here, and I believe I have uncovered the cause of Professor Hardcastle's death. I need officers here in full HAZMAT suits. Make sure to bring one for me and my son too." Dr. Salomon's voice was firm.

"On it," the inspector replied, not caring to hear the details. He thought for a second about leaving the whole mess to the underlings, but he knew his curiosity would keep him involved. His head throbbed as he made the call.

A team, clad in white suits, was in the building promptly twenty minutes after the call. The father and son were also donning their protective attire. No one spoke. Finally, the troop gathered inside the massive office and Dr. Salomon began his narrative.

"I am quite certain the culprit is the golden yellow dart frog. It has enough poison on its skin to paralyze then kill all of us in less than three minutes. The professor had been pointing to the bug on his desk to give us a clue. The planner on his desk records a receipt from a shipment, the black-market type, of rare species from Colombia. This is one of them," he pointed to a shelf above the desk.

"A frog is secured in a cage up there, but the small beetle that I found dead on that desk had visited this frog which fell into that cup of coffee." The room followed Sir Wendel's finger to the stained sides of a coffee cup.

"This, being drunk, revealed the bug at the bottom of the cup. The unfortunate professor dumped it out onto the table. He somehow surmised, likely by the onset of symptoms, what had happened. He recognized the dangerous situation that would arise after his death and during the cleaning out of this room in preparation for an incoming science professor. Thus, the look of horror on his visage, poor man!"

The HAZMAT team transferred one dead bug and one golden yellow dart frog (even though it was quite rare and on an endangered species list), to the mortuary. The sleepy funeral director, in robe and slippers, allowed the incinerator to be used to rid England of a potential peril. All of Professor Hardcastle's works were bagged and boxed until they could be deemed safe to read.

On the ride home, Sir Wendel was thinking about the events that transpired then he spoke, "Son, we have learned a valuable lesson here, haven't we?"

"Yes, Father, if you play with fire, you get burned... or die!"

"I am serious, Son, just a small microgram of the frog's poison coming into contact with a human could wreak havoc to the central nervous system causing a complete shutdown of bodily functions."

"Yes, Father, and how do you know all of this?"

"I skimmed the papers on the professor's desk. I saw a bill of sale with a frog listed on it from Colombia. I also flipped open his book on rare species where a bookmark had been placed. He had begun writing his report on the creature, enough for me to guess at why a coffee-soaked beetle was what he was pointing at."

"Dad, was it a beetle or a bug? If it was a beetle, it was from the Coleopteran order, and if it was a bug, it would be from the order Hemipteran."

"We may never know, Son, we may never know."

CHAPTER 2

Fallacy Revealed

"Bonjour, mon ami!" The cold, sharp edge of panic was in the voice of the *propriétaire*. "This is Jacques from the *Shrimp and Dip* restaurant. I need your assistance, *s'il vous plait!*"

"My son and I have not yet dined, so we will come to your rescue at once, and then partake of your delicious faire. Expect us within ten minutes, *Monsieur!*" Sir Wendel Salomon quickly hung up the phone.

"Winston, we must go! No time to waste. A friend is in need." Dr. Salomon wrapped a scarf around his neck, grabbed an umbrella, and headed for the door. Winston, on the other hand, knowing he had to rush to keep up with his father, carried his shoes and with jacket under his arm prepared for an emergency exit.

Father and son in a gray Mercedes drove the six blocks on damp streets to the posh but poorly named seafood restaurant. Winston tried to get a feel for the predicament from his father but none was to be had.

"No idea of dear Jacques' plight, but he was in a frenzy though. It can't be good. We shall remain undercover, my son, until we ascertain the nature of this crisis. Be cool, calm, and collected so you won't disturb the patrons. We will act as if we are just coming in for our supper."

"I don't need to pretend to be hungry. Let's solve this mystery *tout suite!*" chortled the sixteen-year-old. Dr. Salomon and Winston were met at the door by a thin, well-dressed, wide-eyed man.

"*Bonjour, Monsieur!*" Jacques was overly loud with a forced cheerfulness. Then he whispered, "I cannot allow the customers to know the seriousness of this matter, nor can I allow anyone to leave this establishment!" Beads of sweat were forming upon the man's forehead. He fiddled with the menus while quietly continuing with his narrative.

"Do you see those four magnificently dressed women over there, the table at the center of the room? They have been robbed while sitting at that very table!" Jacques groaned but hid a frown. "When they opened their bags to pay, their money, it was gone. *Mon Dieu!*"

"You do trust them, Jacques?" inquired Dr. Salomon.

"Oh yes, with my life! The one in pink, she is my Great Aunt Claire, my late Grandfather's sister." Jacques was whispering with urgency.

"Do not worry, Jacques, just seat us as close to that table as you can. We will soon be enlightened. Watch the door; let no one exit."

The dim room was not spacious, having only ten round tables. The two largest tables seated eight; three had room for six, and the remainder with room for two. Each table had a white linen tablecloth that fell nearly to the floor.

The four elderly ladies, although recently robbed, did not seem particularly troubled, however poor Jacques was struggling to keep his cheerful, positive persona.

"What can you see, Winston?" Dr. Salomon spoke covertly behind a menu to disguise his intent. Winston also held up his menu and spoke.

"Hmm, nearly every table is filled. At the one closest to us sits a man and wife in their 70's, then to the left is a man eating by himself wearing wrinkled trousers–no wife I suppose. He is reading a little red book and has a nice watch. Let's see, behind me I saw two men, whose likenesses are similar enough that they could be brothers."

Sir Wendel peered over the menu and nodded. Jacques seeing the father and son appearing ready to order, arrived with a basket of rolls and a pitcher of ice water for refills.

"Before you order, may I introduce you to the dear ladies?" asked Jacques nervously.

"A quick question first, Jacques. Do you trust your waiters?" Sir Wendel kept his voice at a whisper.

"Very much, all relatives, all dependent on me, all faithful and true. I assure you!"

The father and son stood and followed Jacques who began the introductions.

"This is my dear Aunt Claire. Auntie, this is Dr. Wendel Salomon and his son, Winston." Her lace covered arm reached out to the Doctor, who took her hand and gently kissed it.

"So pleased to meet you, Sirs. These are my very close and dear friends and have been so since before we could tie our own shoes," she laughed. "We grew up in lovely Paris and I will not tell you how many years ago that has been. This is Cherie, Adelaide, and Clementine." Hands were kissed while expensive French perfume wafted about. Winston's stomach growled.

"We dress up once a year and meet here at my sweet nephew's most excellent restaurant. That is when we allow ourselves the pleasure of remembering the time when we were young and beautiful," the septuagenarian Claire reported.

Winston's thoughts were elsewhere. Behind the table to the right of the single man with wrinkled pants, was a table of eight. It was placed farther away from the other patrons for an obvious reason. There was seated a man and wife with six children; three girls and three boys—all with matching outfits.

The children wore dark blue straw hats with very large brims. The boys wore blue and white suspendered shorts, and the girls wore blue and white suspendered skirts. Winston watched them closely because they did not seem like a typical family. He did realize being raised as an only child may have skewed his opinion, but this family seemed too happy and too good—and were they sextuplets?

"They all looked the same age. It is possible I suppose," thought Winston.

"Ladies," Winston lowered his voice, "may I ask you a question?" They nodded.

"From the time when you sat down until now, did anyone walk behind you to use the loo?"

"Oh, yes," replied Adelaide softly, "that lovely family in the corner. They even came by and greeted us. I am quite sure they have adopted all those beautiful children. Look, they look to be about the same age!" Adelaide turned in her seat to glance again at the perfectly matched children.

"Oh, dear," thought Winston, "nothing like trying to be incognito!"

"Thank you, Ladies." Dr. Salomon bowed slightly, then he and Winston weaved their way back to their table.

"Father, I believe the family is getting ready to leave and I am guessing they will again use the loo. They are the guilty ones; I am sure of it. I have a plan."

The Doctor raised his eyebrows, nodded his head, and made the call to Scotland Yard.

With his father on the phone, Winston watched the mother, and the three matching boys stand up to move toward the loo. After counting to thirty, Winston trailed them into the European-style restroom.

"Ma'am," Winston bellowed, "I see that you have your hands full. Hats off to you for your well-behaved children. We were admiring their behavior, my father and I."

The mother smiled through closed lips. Winston ignored her discomfort.

"Here, I see that you have yet to wash their hands. Let me help you." Before she could protest, Winston hoisted up one of the boys hiding behind his mother, and pumped soap into the his hands.

"I can well see why you were having a time of it; this lad is heavy! Let's see my boy, your straw hat keeps poking me in the eye." Winston set the solid boy down and pulled off the offending hat.

There was an audible gasp in the air and a distinct atmosphere of fear. Winston felt it because he was expecting it. He peered into the hat and his suspicions were correct. He discovered wad of bills laying hidden there. Before anyone could move, two police officers burst through the restroom door and the lad Winston had just set down shouted in a surprisingly deep, manly voice.

"Give me that!" he grabbed for the hat but was too slow.

The first officer quickly grabbed the hatless "boy" by the arm, as the second officer held onto the collars of the other two.

"How dare you!" cried the so-called mother.

"Really, ma'am? How dare you masquerade as family and steal money from four elderly women?" Winston was dismayed.

The officers escorted the 'mother' and matching "boys" out of the loo and toward the front of the store while the patrons looked on curiously. The family's father-figure was waiting in the back of a police van with the three matching girls as a second vehicle awaited the rest of the unusual family.

"I see what we have here." Dr. Salomon's commanding voice hushed them all as he addressed the first 'boy' with the missing hat.

"You are not a child, but a full-grown man from the circus currently performing on the outskirts of town. Dressed like this, you can perform any number of illegal acts. As the four of you walked from your table to the restroom the first time, you crawled unseen under the tablecloth. While beneath the table it was quite a simple task to empty every purse of its cash. When your pretend mother returned, you crawled out and rejoined the others. But since you had to get the money back out of the hat to pay for your dinner, you came back to the restrooms again where my sixteen-year-old son, who had diagnosed this playacting earlier, met you."

The officers hustled the guilty four into the back of the second vehicle and as the door closed the lights went on and the two police vans took off toward the main police station.

Since the money was now evidence to a crime, the elegant ladies received a complimentary meal that night.

"Oh, what a wonderfully sweet man, that Jacques," was Clementine's grateful response.

Later, as Dr. Salmon and his son were served the long-awaited shrimp and fondue dish, they were questioned one more time.

"How did you know they were circus performers masquerading as a family?" asked Jacque.

"On our short drive in tonight," replied Winston, "I saw advertisements for a circus in town, and although they were not covered in clown makeup tonight, there was a set of six trapeze artists of diminutive size on the billboard.

"Yet that resemblance alone did not give it away. There was something more; they had an odd family dynamic of appearing completely perfect. Not a hair out of place, every person in perfectly coordinating clothing. Even the 'mother' and 'father' had an air of perfection about them. It was not a genuine family. A real family is not perfect, even if their clothes match. Children are not cheerful all the time, even if they have smiles. So, what the circus performers actually portrayed came across to us as fake and play-acting. An instant clue to solving the case of the disappearing money."

"And for that, I shall bring you both a *crème brûlée*!" smiled Jacques, not fully understanding the son's conclusion of the matter.

CHAPTER 3

The Oxford Dilemma

Dr. Wendel Salomon reached for the bedside telephone a second too late in the early hours before dawn. An hour later, as he clicked the play button on his answering machine, he heard his son's voice.

"My prof is in need. He will contact you this morning sometime, not my fault."

Sir Wendel groaned; he knew what it likely meant—substitute teaching! He ran through Winston's classes in his head: Algebra, not too bad; British Literature, I can handle that; Soccer, they would never ask me; World History, I like that one; Intro to Philosophy," then out loud he groaned, "I hope not!"

"What, dear?" asked his wife who was rolling out dough for cinnamon rolls.

"Nothing, I was just talking to myself."

Sir Wendel slid the teakettle onto the gas burner and thought about philosophy. It wasn't until he was almost finished with his breakfast and newspaper when the telephone rang with the dreaded call.

"Hello, this is Dr. Salomon speaking."

"Hello, Old Chap! This is Dwight Smythe. I hope you remember me. We were in Professor Morse's sociology class together our senior year."

"Yes, I recall," clipped Sir Wendel.

"Well then, I suppose you know your son is in my Intro to Philosophy class?"

"Of course, I hope he is doing well." Sir Wendel replied while shaking his head.

"An absolutely fine young man, your Winston. You see, my wife is having bunion surgery next week Friday. Would you take my nine-a.m. philosophy class for me? It is 60 minutes, 120 freshmen?"

"Yes, of course." Sir Wendel knew he should add, "With pleasure," but he couldn't lie. They finished the niceties, covered a few classroom details, and Sir Wendel finally hung up the phone.

"What I have feared has come upon me, Ruth. Of all the subjects in the world, philosophy is not the one I ever wanted to dig into again."

"My dear, you will do fine. I am sure of it." Mrs. Salomon promised while refilling his teacup.

Later that morning, Dr. Salmon pulled down the accordion-style ladder in the upstairs hallway which lead to the attic storage area, climbed up and found the box labeled, "Textbooks and Notes." Philosophy was at the bottom, and when he pulled it out, the memories resurfaced.

"Not my forte. I did not enjoy reading ramblings of men who based their ideas on their ideas," Sir Wendel thought. It wasn't that he didn't see the truth in some philosophers' opinions; for philosophy at its beginning was the search for wisdom and the intellectual probing of any subject. But now it had fallen into nothing but contradictions stemming from the confused thoughts of men trying to erase God's existence.

"Time to study," he said aloud while carrying the box down to his den.

Friday arrived and as he drove to the meeting of the minds, Sir Wendel prayed, "God, give me wisdom." Being halfway through the semester, Sir Wendel was prepared for a not totally ignorant group of students. As they came into the amphitheater to take their seats, he cringed slightly and adjusted the collar on the black robe he wore over his suit.

Winston had filed in with the rest of the freshmen and sat in the back row. He slumped down even though his classmates knew this was his famous father. Winston also knew that a philosophical conflict would surely arise. Sir Wendel noticed him in the back and smiled to himself.

Suddenly realizing the room had become quiet, Dr. Salomon began, "Who knows the difference between rhetoric and sophistry?"

The intimidated group, having been clued to the greatness and intelligence of the man before them, said nothing.

"Let us not be afraid to be wrong! Making mistakes makes us wiser and also humbler." Dr. Salomon encouraged.

One lad in the second row raised his hand, "Rhetoric is persuasion towards the truth, and sophistry is persuasion to deceive."

"Great definition. May I add that many a defense lawyer uses that last technique?"

The class snickered, which broke the ice.

"Since you will become what you behold, let us hope in this class you behold truth. We know that there are laws of thought in the same way we have learned the laws of science and the universe. Name three, someone, anyone?" He queried.

More hands were raised.

"Yes, ma'am." Dr. Salomon called out.

A smart-looking girl with large black eyeglasses answered, "The law of gravity?"

"Which is…?"

"What goes up must come down?"

The class giggled.

"And…?" prodded the professor.

"The 1st and 2nd laws of thermodynamics, which are the law of conservation of energy and the law of thermodynamics. In an isolated system, energy is neither created nor destroyed and that entropy always increases," the brave girl answered.

"Entropy is…?"

"The change of movement in the universe from order to disorder," she added, adjusting the frames on her glasses.

"We could continue with the laws of nature, the laws of mathematics or even the laws of God—which would be the Ten Commandments, in case some of you were not aware of those."

Eyebrows raised and Sir Wendel thought to himself, "So it begins!"

"But who knows the laws of thought?" the professor continued.

A boy in the back row touted, "As one thinks in his heart, so is he?"

"Now that is philosophy and scripture! I was wanting the definition of the law of identity, which is: if a statement is true, then it is true. In other words, I cannot, to escape a debate, say that for you the statement is true, but for me it is not. No! Statements cannot be both true and false, which is the law of non-contradiction. You cannot say for instance, that Darwinism is true, but it is also false. That is called wanting to make everyone happy and not caring about truth at all. Also, a statement is either true or false, which is called the law of excluded middle. This means that we cannot have some possibility that falls between true and false. These three laws are the basis for the study of logic. And yes, I do know that this is a philosophy class, but logic is considered to be a branch of philosophy. Logic is concrete and based on the laws of thought. It is an objective reasoning skill. Philosophy is always debated because it is a self-report or a subjective use of logic. It is trying to make one's own ideas seem more plausible, although I do agree that truth can come to the surface when philosophers use logic skills to arrive at conclusions. We begin this study with an open mind that will hopefully and eventually close upon the truth. When two philosophers have opposite or contradictory views, what are the possible truth-values between the two? Anybody?"

The room was silent.

"There are three possibilities, either the first view is true, and the second view is false, or the first view is false and the second view is true or they are both false. Maybe, for example, there is a fourth option, which is the true one.

"Can anyone name two philosophers with opposing philosophies?"

"Sir?" A hand of a student in the third row was held up tentatively in the air. "It seems that Lao-tzu and the Confucian tenets contradict. Taoism is action through inaction and Confucianism has a very active system of belief."

"Good answer, but it could be they both had part of the truth. Sometimes we act. Sometimes we wait. I quote the wisest philosopher of all time, 'Be still' and again, 'Go and tell.' That would be God of course.

"Solomon, a name similar to my own last name, who was also a well-known philosopher, said:

There is a time for everything,
And a season for every activity under the heavens:
A time to be born and a time to die,
A time to plant and a time to uproot,
A time to kill and a time to heal,
A time to tear down and a time to build,
A time to weep and a time to laugh,
A time to mourn and a time to dance,
A time to scatter stones and a time to gather them,

17

A time to embrace and a time to refrain from embracing,
A time to search and a time to give up,
A time to keep and a time to throw away,
A time to tear and a time to mend,
A time to be silent and a time to speak,
A time to love and a time to hate,
A time for war and a time for peace

"I would enjoy spending some time on these ideas. Are there any other contradictory opinions that we know of?" He called on an adult student in the front row.

"How about John Locke and his view that a wise and benevolent nobility, who is well-educated, could help the common good of the common people, versus Machiavelli, who said that one should stay in power at all costs and that virtue was not important. I think he said, 'Better to be feared than loved,' and 'might makes right.'"

Sir Wendel nodded, "A very good example. It is interesting though, that democracy isn't in either option. Out of the philosophers you have studied thus far, which were pro-democracy?"

"Rousseau?" questioned a girl near the rear of the room.

Sir Wendel nodded again, "You are correct. Rousseau did say that when a government has more power it makes humans less moral and creates more inequality. John Adams stated the American constitutional democracy only works when the people are moral. So, do you think when governing people of differing cultures and beliefs then different methods of governance need to be implemented? In other words, can we have a worldwide government option?"

No one answered.

"Does the government's style shape the landscape, or vice versa? Why is it that in some countries, you cannot park a car in an open lot because it will be stolen, and in others, you can park anywhere and never give it a second thought? Is it a cause-and-effect problem?" Sir Wendel gave them a long pause to ponder.

"I think it is a moral issue," remarked the girl with the black glasses. "People, who have no feelings of guilt, create a chaotic culture which then has need of a controlling leader."

"That was a brave statement which few would admit to believing. You could very well have a strong argument for that case. That brings up the question; where does the conscience come from?" continued Sir Wendel.

Silence.

"Maybe how one is brought up: his or her friendships, education, level of income, cultural beliefs, or religion makes a difference? Can a government control these social elements, without it being tyrannical? Socialism believes that a culture without rich or poor would have no thievery. Ridiculous notion as we all know that there are rich kids who steal. What benefit to society would socialism bring?"

Again, there was silence blanketing the room, but this time, students began whipping out their papers and pens to take notes.

"I agree!" The professor grinned, noticing many students were now pondering his points.

"Here is the real reason some philosophers are hit and miss concerning truth. They have no foundation upon which to base their suppositions. Unlike science, which has a scientific method, we have no method of testing the truth of ideas unless we have a universal foundation. Something that is always true, for all time, and under all circumstances. Any thoughts?"

"It would only work if there were a God," resounded an older student.

"I concur. We cannot even agree on the sanctity of life itself, which is supposed to be the basis for our human existence. But if there is a God and he did create us in our mother's womb, then we do have a purpose. Purpose gives us the drive to be moral beings. It may also be the hope of a good afterlife that keeps us searching for the truth. Without a foundation we are like astronauts in a space capsule who do not know up from down and who have no solid footing on which to stand."

"So, what is the purpose of studying philosophy?" A student questioned.

"Again, it is good to have a wide view to narrowly zero in upon the truth and we do find it, don't we? Name a few philosophers who did this well."

"Descartes. 'I think, therefore I am,' proving the existence of the mind," someone answered.

"Yes, and the Bible says the same thing and was written 1500 years before Descartes," recounted Sir Wendel. 'As a man thinks, so is he.'"

"Aristotle," said another student. "He said, 'Doing good proves one is good.'"

"The book of James in the Bible says the same, 'I will show you my faith by my good deeds.'" The professor was now purposefully stepping on toes.

"Buddha said all human suffering stems from the desire for eternal life!" quipped a lad. Some students giggled thinking this would stump the professor.

"Jesus did say if one suffers in the flesh, one would be done with sin. But even being done with sin or desiring an eternal existence does not secure eternal life. The danger of philosophers and their philosophies comes when they 'think, therefore they believe.'

"Coming up with new ideas or religions, no matter how convincing they seem, does not make them true." Sir Wendel

20

continued, "What about the 13ᵗʰ century, Italian born Thomas Aquinas, who logically proved the existence of God with his five logical arguments? In summary, his 'Quinque viae' are: Something had to cause change without itself changing, nothing good can be the cause of itself, something had to be imperishable, something had to be the ultimate good for there to be a judgment toward good, and since behavior differs in non-intelligent objects and this cannot happen be chance– thus God! The universe had to have been created since everything in existence has to have a beginning and a designer.

"This is called the 'First Cause Argument' and all philosophers after Aquinas have wrestled with either trying to prove or disprove his theory. This law shows that the first cause of limitless space must be infinite; of endless time, eternal; of boundless energy, omnipotent; of moral values, moral; of human love, loving; and of life, living.

"Even Einstein, who never believed in God as far as we know, agreed with the Bible, which says that the universe had a beginning, and the universe will have an ending.

"And going back to what it would be like to float in limitless space. We know a few philosophers who went mad because they could not find their footing on a solid foundation. Everything was circular. How can a random, purposeless existence whose beginning came from nothing have a resulting meaning and purpose? Did 'nothing' create the mind of man and that same mind then become aware of there being a past 'something' that existed?

"Research the deteriorating mental health of aging philosophers like Ludwig Wittgenstein, Albert Camus, or even Friedrich Nietzsche.

"Oh my, we have gone over our time. Class dismissed."

CHAPTER 4

The Great Debate

The Oxford University years were full and fun for Wendel and his five friends. They formed a debate club with a closed membership. They met once a week, usually on Friday nights and each Friday they tackled a new and difficult issue. They spent years solving the problems of society and the world. Some very challenging topics lasted several weeks but whether solved or not, after a predetermined amount of time they would move on to a new subject. They became great masters of controlling emotions and passion without being angry. Often, they would switch sides just to keep the atmosphere pleasant and the process unbiased. Their Oxford professors began to see the resulting skills these students were developing, and they all graduated with top marks and high honors.

The natural leader of the group was Wendel Salomon, whom we've already met. Jack Wilbur was a handsome boy whose goal was a law degree. Samuel Reid was a red-headed English Literature buff and Jonathan Rand was determined to receive a seminary degree. Richard Godwin, a naturalist, wanted to travel the world and discover new species of plants and animals and lastly; Francis Cutler, whose goal was to someday be the Dean of Oxford itself.

A tighter group of *compadres* you would not find anywhere. World hunger, socialism, Darwinism, war, and weapons of war–no topic was taboo. Their motto was, "A wide view exposes the narrow truth." Three months before graduation, a topic came up that threw the team into chaos. No sides could be determined, no two thoughts were alike. Emotions flared and, for the first time, emotions flared uncontrollably! That Friday night was the last they would ever attend debate club and it was the last time during the last months before graduation they even spoke.

Years later, on a train ride to Estonia to visit Ruth's ailing mother, Sir Wendel relayed this story to his wife and to his son, Winston. He had hoped to impart a lesson to Winston and maybe even to gain perspective as he heard himself relate the details of this painful past. His mother-in-law's illness and the rumble of the train caused not just contemplation, but an old feeling to resurface. He had felt it before while riding this same train; it was the same loneliness that had shook him 25 years earlier. He did realize that when his friends parted from each other they were all fearful of what the future would hold and that they dreaded the breaking up of these close friendships. The emotions were caused from knowing they would need to separate from each other and separating in anger was easier than separating from grief. Human psychology had taught him that much.

"What in the world was the big issue being discussed?" Winston's question broke the silent moment of soul searching.

"Ah that, well, you may find it rather silly now, and I quite agree. No laughing, Son." Winston smiled and nodded.

"The issue was whether women should be allowed to receive degrees at Oxford. Now I know it was ridiculous, women had been receiving degrees there for over 40 years at

Oxford's Somerville College for women, and I believe Dorothy Sayers was the first. You read her books didn't you, Winston?"

Winston nodded. The father continued, "Old ideas die hard and nearly all of our fathers had been Oxford graduates and had passed on some of their prejudices to us."

"It sure doesn't seem like a very good issue to debate. There was no going back and changing anything. It wasn't a problem to be solved. Why?" asked Winston.

"You are right, and now I think I know why. All six of us had been so busy, so engrossed in our group, our studies, and our good grades, that we ignored the female presence at Oxford. When we did start taking notice, figuring we would have to eventually find a wife–it hit us like a ton of bricks. We tried to get dates to no avail. We were awkward and because of the fast-approaching shove into the real world, we became obsessed. We could not believe that we had wasted so much time in thought and none in engaging in the real world of relationships. It was a miracle that I met your mother."

"Yes, he was rather awkward!" Ruth Salomon remarked.

Ignoring the jab, Sir Wendel continued, "Jack insisted women should only go to women's colleges and only for nurses training and teaching certificates. I think he was the most frustrated of the bunch. Samuel said that women should go to a women's college if it was clear that they would not marry, so limit it to women over 35. He obviously couldn't get a date. Francis was rather more progressive and said women should not only be allowed, but everything should be equal. Jonathan had frowned and declared that the temptation that the opposite gender brought to campus was deplorable. He felt that they should be separated until after graduation. Ha, the others had stopped arguing when they heard that one. No one in the group had been tempted, except for maybe Jonathan." Sir Wendel smiled at the memory, "Richard had scoffed that by graduation pretty girls would have lost their appeal. What a ludicrous idea!"

"What about you, Dad?"

"I never really remarked about it or rather never felt the willpower to shout louder than the lot of them, so I didn't try. It is easier I suppose to focus on studies without the distraction of the females. But Son, the Bible says that we are to treat all younger women as sisters. Even though you haven't had the pleasure of having a sister, I think you can imagine it. So being surrounded by 'sisters',one is never distracted, but learns how to get along and can practice developing the honor and respect the opposite sex deserves. Having the sister-type friendship takes the mystery out of the relationship, and out of those developing friendships can emerge a lifelong partnership! Monks in caves can be just as distracted with a thought life that isn't focused and disciplined. I think women should be allowed to follow God's path for their lives. Who am I to butt in and give my measly opinion about someone else's life? They belong to God, and they are someone else's daughter and someday maybe, someone's wife!"

"Good point, Dad." Winston began to study the landscape once again.

"Ruth, I have a wonderful idea. When we arrive back home, I am going to have a Swiss Alp reunion with the old pals from the debate group. Time for reconciliation!"

Eight months later, six graying or balding men and one 17-year-old sat around a table enjoying the beautiful summer afternoon on a chateau balcony. The men were catching up with one another. One embarrassing subject was never breached, and slowly the ice between them melted and they laughed heartily together once again.

Jack had married a professor of nursing at London University, no children, but was surrounded by his students. He was the professor of Ethics and Philosophy at the same university where his wife taught. Samuel had never married, but Winston noted that he kept his trousers ironed. He was still in rather good shape because he rode his bicycle to work every day. He was headmaster at a private school for boys and looked it too. Winston avoided the eyes of the strict-looking man. Francis had been married thrice, but soon settled down.

"This one's a keeper," he had remarked glowingly. He had family money, so he spent his time sailing and golfing.

Jonathan was a cleric, had a lovely wife who had been a childhood friend. They had seven children, all with bouncy blonde curls. A picture was passed around. Richard had written several books on the rare species found in exotic places in the world. He had traveled extensively and seen much. He talked of those happy glory days at Oxford but never revealed much about his recent history. Richard spoke little of his wife or family, but sadness showed on his face.

They had gotten quite caught up when the waitress, who brought them tea and biscuits, caught Samuel's eye. Winston noticed and nudged his dad.

Sir Wendel's eyes twinkled with mischief as he asked the waitress, "Ma'am, what do you think is the most important thing in life?"

The waitress smiled a dazzling smile. "Well, I suppose it would be taking joy in all the little moments, which leads to true happiness."

She walked away and Samuel rose quickly to follow her inside. Winston and his father smiled.

CHAPTER 5

The Truth Hurts!

"Hey, Mark, come look at this! Hurry!" Donald Wilson shouted from the couch.

A portly man in his fifties stumbled into the room wearing his nighttime attire.

"What!" Mark grumbled at being disturbed, "you woke me up!"

"Hey, man, it's nearly noon. Anyway, look at this gal on the telly. I used to date her in college and now she is a famous actress! I can't believe it!" Donald was sitting on the edge of his seat in utter amazement.

"Too bad she broke up with you, you could be rich right now." Mark Westcott muttered as he turned to go back to bed.

"I broke up with her," was the reply.

"You are kidding me! Why?"

"She wasn't pretty enough, I guess. I was really cool back then. I remember sitting across the table from her in the library and telling her we were through, that I had found someone else.

Can't remember who that was though. She got up and walked away." The memory was rather painful.

"What a dummy!" Mark declared as he exited the room.

The two men were rooming together while going through divorce proceedings. Mark's was nearly finalized but Donald's was just six months into it. They worked together as mechanics at the largest automobile fix-it shop in town. They both had the day off, which was rare because it was a Saturday–usually the day when the shop was slammed with work.

"I'm going for a walk!" Thirty-year-old Donald bellowed as he slipped on shoes and a coat. Walking was not something he ever did for pleasure, but he suddenly felt closed in and claustrophobic. He glanced around the disorderly room shaking his head at the pile of dishes in the sink, beer cans on the coffee table and floor, and at the black smudged kitchen floor from grease monkey's shoes.

"Mark is such a slob!" he exclaimed under his breath as he walked out.

Not caring where he went, and out of habit, he headed toward his place of employment. His head was down, and he stared at the sidewalk. It wasn't surprising that he bumped hard into someone, sending a startled man's umbrella flying.

Quickly retrieving it, Donald apologized, "So sorry sir, here is your umbrella. I wasn't watching where I was going–hey, you look familiar. I am sure I know you from somewhere. My name is Donald Wilson."

"My name is Wendel Salomon, and I just dropped my car off to get the oil changed and am off for a walk. Want to join me?" Donald took the invite and left with the courteous and forgiving gentleman.

"I noticed that you seemed a bit down in the dumps, Donald?" queried Wendel Salomon.

"Oh, it's been a trying six months, my wife left me, my roommate, Mark, is a complete slob, and I'm just plain unhappy. I'm sure you don't want to hear about it."

"If you want to talk, I would love to listen. Please tell me your story."

Donald proceeded to pour out his complaints and misery to the stranger. They passed a small café and Sir Wendel offered to buy him lunch. They sat at a small table and the waitress brought menus. The conversation was put on pause until after they had ordered.

"I'll take the double cheeseburger with fries and a chocolate milkshake," ordered Donald.

"I'll take a salad and a cup of tea," followed the older and wiser, Sir Wendel.

The conversation commenced.

"My wife just wouldn't listen and didn't understand the kind of stress I was under at work. She didn't give a reason for leaving, she just left me high and dry. I don't want to burden you with my problems, but it does feel good to get this off my chest."

"No problem, Donald. I have a proposition for you. I am somewhat of a counselor, and I think I can help get you through this rough patch in your life."

Donald glanced up, "Really?"

"We can meet here once a week and each time I will give you one thing to do for the week. Nothing hard, I promise. I think you will find that these tasks will pull you out of the doldrums and get you past this trying time."

Sir Wendel paused to see if Donald would agree to the deal.

"You see, Donald, this plan is taken from a verse in the Bible that says, 'If you are willing and obedient, you will eat of the good of the land,' which means success."

"Sure, I can do anything for a week, let's give it a go!"

Already Donald's attitude was perking up as his mind began rising to the challenge.

"OK, here is my card, call me with a time you are available next Saturday, any time of the day, and we will meet here."

The food arrived at that moment and not much was said while the meal was being consumed. Donald finished in half the time it took Sir Wendel. As he slurped up the remaining milkshake, he asked, "What's my first assignment?"

"This week I want you to keep your apartment spotless. Do not say a word to your roommate, and do not do this task in an irritated manner. Be cheerful and yes, clean up after your roommate, Mark is his name? Do the dishes, make both beds, et cetera. It is just for one week." Sir Wendel saw the horror on Donald's face.

"You are kidding me! No offence, but yuck!" Donald sputtered.

"You decide, Donald, and if you do this, give me a call and we will meet."

Sir Wendel rose, left a tip, paid for the meal, and headed back to retrieve his vehicle.

Donald sat quietly, still reeling with the thought of cleaning up after Mark. It was the last thing he had expected. Though he didn't have any idea what he expected.

"What a stupid idea. Who does he think he is!" thought Donald. He glanced down at the card he had been given and received the second surprise of his day:

Sir Wendel Salomon Ph. D.
Professor, University of Oxford

As he made his way back home, Donald had a decision to make. He was not willing to do the task nor willing to be obedient, and he knew it. Walking into the apartment was just plain depressing, but instead of sitting down, ignoring the mess, and watching television, he began picking up the living room. He wiped down the coffee table, swept the floor, dusted the television then moved on to the kitchen. He washed the dishes and cleaned out the refrigerator, getting rid of several questionable leftovers. He then cleaned out the caked-on build-up in the microwave. After two hours, he moved on to his bedroom. He heard Mark shut the front door and was glad he didn't have to explain his actions just yet.

After doing his laundry at the coin-op down the hall and finishing his bedroom, it was nearly 5:00 and his stomach growled. He also growled when he walked into his roommate's bedroom. Not wanting to invade the man's privacy too much, he only carried out the three armloads of dishes to the sink, dumped old food and three-dozen beer cans into the trash. He then washed a final load of bed sheets and towels. At 8:00 pm after he had finished making the beds and sweeping and mopping floors, he had really wanted to quit. Instead, he tackled the worst room in the 800 square foot apartment— the bathroom! He did it and he did it well. The room smelled like a Clorox advertisement.

At 10 pm, he washed the remaining dishes, put them away, and took out five bags of rubbish. He then went to the corner store and rewarded himself with a hot dog and a soda. He tried watching TV, but he was so tired he crawled into bed, smiled at the clean sheets, and conked out.

Donald spent his week working hard at ignoring his feelings about cleaning up after Mark, but by that Friday, even Mark started being aware and was working at keeping the place tidy.

"You don't have to clean up after me, Donald. You're not my mother!"

"Or wife," Donald added, "I know, but it is making me feel better, not so focused on myself. It has been an experiment and I think it's working." He immediately dialed the phone number on the card.

"Sir Wendel? I did it! I would like to meet tomorrow if you can. Oh, this is Donald, we met last Saturday?"

"Sounds great," was the happy reply, "what time?"

"I work at 9:00, how about we meet at 8:00? I work at the shop you took your car to. It's just down the street from the café."

The next day, Sir Wendel was eating his English muffin and drinking his tea, while Donald was eating his bacon and scones while they discussed Donald's week.

"Are you ready for your next assignment?" asked the professor.

"I'm ready, it can't be any worse than what I went through last week!" he laughed.

"I want you to send your alienated wife a note of appreciation every day. Be specific and be thankful." He pulled out a bag and took out a page of stationary, a pen, and a stamped envelope.

"We can start right now."

Obediently, Donald wrote:

Dear Matilda,

I wanted to write and tell you how much I appreciated the work you did to keep our house clean. After living with a slovenly roommate, I realize how much I took you for granted and I am sorry for that.

Sincerely,

Donald

He had the professor read it over then he put it in the envelope, sealed it, and added the address.

"Here you go, Donald." Sir Wendel handed him a bag containing a week's worth of stationery, stamps, and envelopes.

"You make it easy for me, Professor!" the grateful man declared.

"Out of curiosity, are you going to keep your place clean now, or is it going to go back to being a bachelor pad?" smiled Sir Wendel.

"No sir, even Mark is shaping up. I think I'm a new man!"

After dropping the note into the mailbox, Donald arrived home that night after work. His place sparkled. He plopped down on the sofa with a much-needed time of relaxation. But he could not find the remote control to the TV. He looked under the couch.

"Reminder: sweep under the couch." He groaned to himself. He lifted the cushions and was startled. There were coins, popcorn, wrappers, forks, and spoons and... Dirt! He could not believe what he had been sitting on for who knows how long. Did his wife always clean out from under cushions and underneath the couch? She must have. He sat and wrote his second note for the next day's mail:

Dear Matilda,

I am looking for the controller and realized that you must have kept the underneath of the couch and cushions clean. I never noticed how much you did to keep things in order. I am sorry and thank you for being such a hard worker.

Donald

Donald gave up on watching the television partly because he still couldn't find the controller and watching TV without a controller was no fun, and partly because he spent forty-five minutes cleaning under the cushions and under the couch. He washed up and fell into bed. His hand touched something under his pillow, the controller!

Donald faithfully and promptly mailed a note each day to his estranged wife. Sometimes he wrote two at a time. He thanked her for the food she had made, especially the meatloaf with the tiny bits of carrots in it. He said he realized how much work it was to get those pieces that small. Then he thanked her for doing the laundry and hanging up his shirts right out of the drier. He wrote that it took him months before he realized why his clothes had been so wrinkled. He sent one thanking her for the past birthday and Christmas presents she had given to him; he had thought of it while using the electric razor he had asked her for. He sent one in appreciation for mopping the floor and apologized for tracking in so much grease from the mechanic shop. He then thanked her for working at the dry cleaners. He had read an article that told how dangerous the chemicals could be to a person. He said he was sorry that he couldn't have provided better for her. In that envelope he sent $200 and said he had hoped that by next payday he could send more. He wrote two that day. The second was an apology for the times he had lost his temper, for hogging the TV controller, for never asking what she wanted to watch, and for leaving his socks lying about. He said he hoped someday she would be able to forgive him.

On Thursday, he received a letter from her! She simply thanked him for the letters, and she accepted his apologies and then updated him on her personal news. She had quit her job at the dry cleaners to care for her mother full-time, as she was now completely bedridden. Donald put down the letter and suddenly realized how selfish he had been. He rang the professor, made the Saturday appointment for noon, and finished the day with a bowl of Campbell's cream of mushroom soup made with water. It was the only thing left in the cupboards.

The week's details were conveyed to the professor, and the note from his wife was shared.

"I feel so badly that I didn't care enough to keep in touch with her. I was so hurt that I didn't see that she was hurt." Donald shook his head.

"I am proud of you, Donald. Godly sorrow is all about wanting relationships to be healed, but regret doesn't accomplish anything. Let's move on. This week isn't going to be so cut and dried. In other words, I am not going to tell you what to do, you will tell yourself."

Donald looked confused.

"There are three parts of your being that makes the whole of who you are: your body, your soul, and your spirit. Unless all three are healthy, you aren't really a healthy person. Let's take your body first. How many vegetables do you eat in a day?"

Donald nearly laughed out loud, "None, not since I lived with my mom." He glanced down at his half eaten grilled cheese sandwich, fries, and milkshake.

"I am not criticizing you, Donald. I am trying to give you a new possibility for yourself. How much physical exercise do you get in a week?"

Donald squirmed, "None."

"Do you do anything to ensure the ongoing health of your body?"

"Well, I don't smoke anymore, gave that up six years ago. The wife didn't like it."

"Good man. This week I want you to focus on your body and everything you put into it and everything you do to it. Do it purposefully with focus. Do not be a passive participant in life—be engaged."

Donald nodded.

"Now, your soul includes your mind, your will, and your emotions. Your mind will also be your focus this week. What can you do to enlarge your mind?"

"You mean read books?"

"Maybe, if they are worthy books. But also, and more importantly, do not allow any negative thoughts to rule your mind, either about yourself, others, or about your situation. You are not a failure, and you are not a victim. Think success and progress. We are all on a journey and we are all in a process. It is time to engage." Again, Donald nodded.

"Lastly, if you do not feed your spirit, you will be lacking in the major character qualities of love, joy, peace, patience, kindness, long suffering, gentleness, and humility. You do this only by connecting to God, the one that created you and created you for a purpose. Submit to him by accepting what He has given to all of us, the gift of forgiveness through what his son, Jesus, did by dying for our sins. We have to accept his sacrifice, or it won't apply to our own freedom from guilt and shame."

Donald nodded again.

"Here are the notes from today and a Bible. I must run. See you next Saturday." He paid the tab and left.

"Wow that was heavy!" Donald pondered as he finished his lunch.

After work, he walked a different direction and found himself knocking on the door of the house he hadn't seen in six months. Matilda answered.

"Hi, Matilda, I came to visit your mom. Hope I'm not bothering you; I am just so sorry that she is suffering!"

"Come in, I know she will be pleased to see you."

The circles under her eyes, something Donald would not have noticed before, shook him. He slipped off his shoes and went into the mother-in-law's bedroom.

"Matilda, if you have shopping or something you need to do, go ahead. I'll stay until you get back."

"Thank you. I do need to pick up a few things." She quickly left.

"Hi, Mom, how are you feeling?"

"Donald, I have missed you! Where were you yesterday?"

"At work, as usual."

"My legs hurt so badly. I can't sleep."

The aging woman had gone downhill since he had seen her last. He offered to rub her feet and was surprised at how swollen they were. While he rubbed her feet and ankles, he told her about the nice professor and all the things he had taught him and how he was learning to be a better person. She smiled.

"Yes, dear, and don't forget to take out the garbage. You know how the dog likes to get into it; such a mess he makes." The woman weakly voiced. She was somewhere in the past, but soon dropped off to sleep. Donald went into the kitchen and opened the refrigerator. He would have normally grabbed something to eat, but now it felt like stealing. He glanced at the end of the counter and saw the pile of letters he had sent. He was so grateful that he had done that. Matilda's pain, he realized, had been much greater than his.

He sat at the table, read through the professor's notes, which included a prayer.

"God, I don't deserve anything from you, but please forgive me of all my selfishness. I accept your gift of forgiveness and freedom from guilt and shame. Please take care of Lorna, make her legs better. Thank you. Amen."

Matilda walked in and he helped her with the groceries.

He noticed that she held the day's mail; his latest note was on top.

"She's sleeping. I rubbed her feet and ankles, and she drifted off thinking I was your dad. I am going to try to come every day so you can have a break, if that's okay?"

"Thank you, that would be lovely," she answered.

Donald slipped out and felt good. He didn't just walk home—he jogged. And he jogged every day that whole week. He ate vegetables and gave up soda, fries, and shakes. He dug out a set of dumbbells from his closet and lifted weights while watching television. He wouldn't allow himself to sit down. He started reading the Bible the professor had given him. Every day after work he gave Matilda a break and sat with Lorna.

On Friday, his day off that week, Donald went to the barber. He got a short haircut and a shave. He bought more fruit and veggies at the corner market and went home and made a veggie omelet, even Mark had some.

"Wow, Donald, you look great. What's gotten into you?"

"I've been on a journey of self-discovery that started when I ran into a professor. Do you want to hear about it?" For two hours Donald told Mark the entire story of his reclamation. Mark himself became convicted of wasting his life and took the Professor's notes and promised himself that his journey was beginning.

When Donald met Sir Wendel early the next morning. Sir Wendell didn't even recognize him.

"You've lost weight and hair! You look good. Tell me about your week."

Donald told him about his mother-in-law, his wife, and about Mark.

"It was an amazing week. I prayed, I read the Bible you gave to me, I ate well and exercised. Professor, I cannot thank you enough!" Tears were welling up in his eyes.

"What's my next assignment?"

"Donald, no more assignments unless they come from God. This is the last time we will meet. I will keep you and yours in my prayers but keep me posted. I'm planning a trip to Siberia so I may be gone for a month. But you can mail me a note now and then."

They finished their tea, shook hands, and parted ways. Sir Wendel received a thank you note a week later and an update a month after that. Both Donald and Mark had been reunited with their families and both were changed men.

While Donald was moving some belongings back into his mother-in-law's house, he passed the local bookstore. There in the window was Sir Wendel's face on a book entitled, *Sometimes Being Right is Wrong*, subtitled, *Or Sometimes Being Smart is Foolish.*

"So that is where I had seen him before!" Donald smiled.

CHAPTER 6

The Process of Elimination

Sir Wendel began once again to diligently research Siberia. Interruptions are annoying to the intellectual, and no more than an hour into the solitude of his study, the phone rang.

"Yes, this is Professor Salomon. How can I help you?" He tried not to sound curt.

"This is Bradley Scott at Oxford, I'm sorry to bother you, Professor. I have a problem that is worrisome. It isn't that I cannot ignore it, for I could, but I'm troubled and need advice."

"I am all ears," encouraged the professor relaxing a bit.

"I completed my research paper on John Locke's definition of equal rights. I finished it last night and it was in a folder on my desk. When I got up, it was gone!" groaned Bradley Scott.

"Who has keys to your room?" asked Sir Wendel.

"My roommate, John Lock. I would have noticed if he had turned on a light."

"Odd that he shares the name of the great philosopher that you wrote about! What is he like, this roommate?" asked Sir Wendel.

"He's a quiet sort, stays to himself, doesn't talk much, and I don't think he has friends."

"It would be easy to steal a key and to have another made. Do you have your key now?" asked the professor.

"Yes, I have it right here."

"Did you see John leave this morning?"

"Yes."

"Could he have had your essay among his possessions when he left?"

"I don't think so, I stayed in bed but was awake and was aware of his movements and saw him leave. I don't think he would have taken the risk."

"Did he get up during the night?"

"Not sure."

"Do you snore? If you were snoring, he would know you were asleep."

"Yes, I guess so, my brother used to wake me up to stop the noise."

"What did he carry out with him this morning?"

"His literature textbook, a pen, and a notebook. He doesn't carry much at a time; I think he is rather weak."

"Does he have duct tape? Look on his desk," ordered Sir Wendel.

"Yes, how did you know?" asked the bewildered Bradley.

"He could have used the tape to conceal the essay."

"Where could something be hidden in your room?" Before the boy could answer, the professor continued. "Look underneath both of your mattresses."

"Ok, Nothing."

"Look in his closet, and make sure your door is locked."

"Nothing."

"How about taped under his desk?"

"Nope."

"Go to his closet again. Was it left open when he left?"

"Yes."

"Does he usually leave his closet door open?"

"No, never."

"Reach up above the door on the inside and see if you feel anything."

"Yes," came the shocked voice. "I feel a plastic bag, tape over it, adhering it to the wall, and here are my papers, wrapped up. Yes, I am quite sure! You are a genius, Professor!"

"Son, stop! Do not remove the bag just yet. I want you to stay inside of your room with the door locked until I get there. Something sinister is going on and I am afraid you could be in danger." The professor's voice was sharp and serious.

"The paper is due next period; it will be late if I don't get it there in time!" complained Bradley.

"I understand, but I have an 'in' with the Dean and will most certainly get you off the hook. Only open the door to my son, Winston. I am going to pull him out of class and send him right over. Hold tight. I'll be there in twenty minutes. What room are you in?"

"504."

Dr. Salomon hung up, grabbed his coat, and dialed the university's security department. He passed on some instructions to them. He then paged his son with the number 505 which meant 'SOS', their code between them. Once Winston found a phone and called the answering service, the message would send him over to the fifth floor, room 504, telling him to be undercover, wary, and watchful, and to announce himself to Bradley Scott and to keep the door locked.

Winston received the page, tried to creep out of class, but ended up having to tell the professor he had an emergency. He made the call then ran to the fifth floor and remembered that he had a friend on that floor that slept through first period, sometimes second. He rapped on room 511 then walked in. His buddy lay snoring. Winston crossed the room and flew open the window to see if his dad had arrived yet. He had a great view of the parking lot. Leaving the door slightly ajar, he quickly ran down the hall carrying books to seem like he was on his way to class in case someone came up from the stairwell. Winston rapped on the door and announced, "Bradley Scott, this is Winston Salomon, my dad is on his way!" Bradley opened the door.

"I am not sure why your dad is taking this so seriously; he has me spooked."

"My dad is a genius, and if he senses something isn't quite right, it's best just to listen to him."

Winston waited ten more minutes, got antsy, and told Bradley he was going to run down the hall to see if his dad had arrived.

"Keep the door locked. I will knock three times when I get back."

Winston ran back to room 511, peering out the window just in time to see his dad running at full speed toward the dorms. He was met by the campus police officer. Satisfied, Winston burst out of the door in time to see a dark figure slip into room 504.

"Oh, no! They must have knocked three times! I blew it!"

He had an idea for making amends. He rushed down the hall. Luckily the person hadn't locked the door behind him. Winston burst into the room and there were three boys standing with shocked looks on their faces.

"Hey, Bradley, who are your friends? I think I left my books in here. Ah, there they are. Aren't you going to be late for class, come on and let's go!"

"He isn't going anywhere right now, we have a transaction between us, like a deal." One of the boys awkwardly retorted.

It was obvious that these freshmen were ignorant. He recognized two of them.

"OK, I will wait outside."

He moved slowly, gathering up books, trying to stall for time.

Professor Wendel then flew into the room with the campus policeman right behind him. One of the boys passed out, one started crying, and the other slumped to the floor.

"What is going on here?" The policeman demanded loudly.

"Let me handle this, Officer. If you wouldn't mind stepping outside, I think I can figure out this scenario." The policeman wasn't happy, but he obliged.

After the boys were seated on the bed, he asked the boy who seemed the least nervous to explain.

"We joined this club; it is called *The Gullivers* after the book *Gulliver's Travels*. We usually remember Gulliver as being the giant, but no one remembers him as the tiny man bullied by the giant little girl." Wendel nodded and worked to keep a straight face.

"See, since none of us are popular, smart, or good looking, we have no friends. Then this guy came up to each of us and asked if we wanted to join his club. Well of course we all were thrilled. Finally, we could be a part of something. He said we had to pass an initiation ritual, which was to steal someone's finished essay and bring it to him. That's why we did it. I thought Bradley would be in class when we came in here to take his paper. We are sorry–so sorry, Bradley. I'm not a very good roommate."

"What is this fellow's name?" asked Sir Wendel.

The boys looked at each other, "We were sworn to secrecy."

"How many in the group?"

"We don't know. This was our initiation. We are to meet at midnight by the pond."

Sir Wendel stood up, "This is what we are going to do. You take Bradley's paper since we can print out another. We will set up a sting operation tonight, but boys, this is your only chance not to get expelled from school. You follow along. We only want the leader or leaders, and you won't even have a record. I have a suggestion for you when this is all over." He reached into the closet and ripped the packet down. The boys looked surprised.

"Take this. Don't act suspicious. Don't talk to each other. We will see you at midnight."

The three boys left.

"Let's get your floppy disk. I will go personally and print it off then turn it in for you." Sir Wendel offered Bradley.

"You don't have to, sir!" Bradley turned a bit pink from embarrassment.

"No, I will, plus I am looking forward to reading it."
Winston and his dad left the room. "The leaders of these kind of bullies gain control by having the underlings break rules and laws

44

to gain power over them," explained the father. Wendel talked to the security team, filled them in on the particulars and planned to meet them at midnight behind the bushes. He then printed off the paper, read it, and after explaining the situation to the boy's professor, handed it over.

"Time for a nap. Kids can get away with little sleep, but I can't anymore." Wendel thought as he drove home. At midnight the stage was set and right on time a group of seven boys gathered in a circle. Two of them handed over papers, and they were told to kneel. As soon as the four new boys knelt, police came from every direction.

No one escaped. The three boys that didn't kneel were arrested and put in the holding area until Scotland Yard could be notified. The other boys were shaken. Sir Wendel gave them a lecture about honor and privilege. He then told them they would be off the hook on one condition, that they would meet him the next day at noon in the library. They happily agreed.

The library was awe-inspiring. One never grew tired of gazing at the wooden shelves, beautiful scrollwork, the long rows of books, and the artistry on the ceiling. They found a quiet side room where they all gathered. Bradley Scott had also been invited; five members, a pretty good start.

"I have been thinking that a club needs to be started that would begin to debate the issues of the day. Here is a book on policy debate. It is useful to start with and I would like to come every Friday to hear your results. Our first debate subject is contained in Bradley Scott's paper on the definition of equal rights. I think it is a good start. Listen to a few points here. John Locke, not the one sitting among us, believed in equal rights under the law. He believes that all humans had the right to 'life, liberty, and estate.' Of course, you know that in the American constitution, instead of estate it reads 'happiness', and that was because of the hotly contested issue of slavery. The slaves were considered part of one's estate. And we know that people are not to be owned but have the innate right to be free."

The boys were staring blankly, and Sir Wendel came back to the topic at hand.

"Some possible debate questions you could choose from are: should it be our right to pass on to our children what we possess when we die? Is it our right to snuff out a life for any reason? Is liberty a right we have at the expense of someone else's liberty? For example, you may have the liberty to shout obscenities on a street corner, but then I lose my right NOT to hear them, and finally, do all people deserve equal rights regardless of their behavior? Well then, boys, here are the papers, and here are the questions I wrote. I will see you next Friday night about 9 o'clock, this same place?"

The boys blinked and nodded, and that was the beginning of 'Gulliver's Club' a very logical debate club. The amazing result was that fifteen groups started that year and Sir Wendel had to take turns visiting them all. Some met on Saturday nights so he could do double time.

"How was your meeting at the library, Dear?" asked Mrs. Ruth Salomon when he climbed into bed that night.

"Quite amazing! A bit like destiny I think," he replied.

CHAPTER 7

The Sherlock Performance

Sir Wendel Salomon, even though he was on a sabbatical from teaching at Oxford University, was kept too busy for his liking. His favorite pastimes were study and research. It had been months since his last opportunity to relax and dig deep into topics he enjoyed. The timing always had to be just right, and distractions brought to a minimum. While sitting in his office armchair meditating on whether this would be a good time to prepare for his long-anticipated trip to Russia, his phone rang. Not the home phone, which his wife could have answered, but his cellular phone, which few had the number for.

"Oh bother," he complained.

The caller was one of Winston's old high school teachers. It was a classically based school that still taught Latin, logic and astronomy. Winston was long gone, but this teacher had kept the number. Mr. Arbuckle, a very excited younger man, had come up with an idea for his Logic class. He wanted Dr. Salomon to be a guest speaker in three weeks for an hour, dressed as Sherlock Holmes. Any topic that was logic-based was acceptable for the thirty senior level students. The Doctor agreed, but made it clear he did not like the whole dressing up bit.

When the call was over, he immediately went to his wife, Ruth, to complain, mostly because she would always offer cheerful encouragements. She thought the idea was brilliant and set to work making the costume. He set to work on what in the world he would be saying. It was never easy preparing for a class, even a subject that one taught year after year. Sir Wendel loved to add a spark to his lessons and never wanted precious topics like logic to seem dry and boring.

Three weeks passed by all too quickly and he found himself holding a pipe, wearing a strange hat and cape, and feeling ridiculous while standing in front of a class of snickering teenagers.

He began, "If the motive of rightness and smartness is pride and selfishness, then the motive is a false one. Rightness and smartness need to have a foundation of humility and love. Some of you will be doctors or lawyers, and maybe a few in here will be politicians. You may be proud of your accomplishments, and yet your own personal life could end up looking like the underbelly of the dark streets of London. I am telling the truth. How many times have I been visited at 221B Baker Street by the most important, the richest, the best dressed in all of London, only to hear a story of utter depravity! Many times, I tell you, as Dr. Watson could attest to if he had been available today."

The professor started pacing the room, getting into character. The students stopped snickering and watched Sir Wendel as if watching a movie picture.

"You think, my dear fellows that the law, obeying the law, a good heritage, and a flawless lifestyle will keep you permanently from the pitfalls of life. Can you avoid the dark night of the soul or the wretched addictions that ravage one's life until there is barely life to salvage? Can you, by an act of your will, be happy and make the others around you happy? No, my dear sirs, and I will prove it! The study of words using the Greek language reveals deeper meanings than our own English ones. Take the word 'love' for example. One word for love in Greek is 'eros' where we get the word erotic. The Greeks looked at this type of love as one that was dangerous and irrational and being out of control. They did not look at this passion and desire as a positive idea like we do today. 'Madly in love' was interpreted more like 'crazy without reason'!

"'Philautia,' as the Greeks so named it, is a love that is a basic self-love with two sides. One side is a narcissistic love that obsesses about one's own fame and fortune. The other side of this love 'philautia' is a healthy version, where one is secure in himself or herself and is able to love others. As Jesus said, 'Love your neighbor as yourself', or as Aristotle put it, 'All friendly feelings for others are an extension of a man's feelings for himself'.

"Another meaning for the word love is 'phileo'. This is the loyal, friendship love that Aristotle himself proposed, which requires a certain virtue, equality, and closeness. But when this love is strained, and someone in the relationship fails to give equally, phileo may fail. So, a marriage based on eros and phileo, could be in error and may fail.

"There is also 'storge' love, which is a family love. This is the kind of love you can bank on if your parents are somewhat normal. There is no stronger love on earth than a mother for her child, and strong still is a father's love for his offspring. This 'storge' is a devoted, family love that brings joy to the heart of the one who is loving, a man for his wife, a wife for her husband, a parent for child or someone for his dog. This love feels good. It is a love based on relationship and carries a certain joy and a commitment.

"But this love has responsibilities, and when one's spouse or child becomes so offensive that the relationship is broken, the good times seem forgotten.

"Lastly, there is 'agape', a word not found often other than the 120 times in the New Testament of the Bible. Agape was translated into Latin as 'caritas' where we get the word 'charity'. C.S. Lewis called this 'gift-love'. It is a love for everyone, from stranger to family. This is a one-way love based on nothing more than another's existence. This love cannot be removed. Who in this room has this kind of love?"

The students were exceptionally silent, and Mr. Arbuckle didn't seem very happy. He wasn't planning on religion being mentioned. Dr. Sherlock was enjoying his moment.

"So, you probably would agree then that every shred of love that you have for each other: parents, teachers, girlfriends, or boyfriends, is completely and totally self-gratifying based on whether the other person treats you right, makes you happy, meets your needs— emotionally and physically?"

The class shifted in their seats, wishing the speech was over.

"Logic is an interesting study because no matter how clever we get; we cannot change our character. No matter how much we win an argument, we cannot win friends using arguments. What then can be done for our pathetic state-of-being? Love is the biggest fallacy of all time, and now you can see why. If you could take the temperature of our culture, you would see that over the past forty years, the love levels of the 'agape' kind has failed. It feels cold out there, students! What can we do? Is there hope? This may be the greatest mystery ever solved and I intend to solve it.

"Watson is going to join me Friday night, at 9 o'clock at the Oxford University library, I invite you to join us. We will solve this case! Class." He tipped his cap and left the room and the building.

Sir Wendel was certain that Mr. Arbuckle wasn't going to send him a thank you note. Just in case someone showed up at the Friday night debate club at the library, he had to be prepared. He rang his devout Catholic friend, Brother Thomas, who looked the part of Dr. Watson, and filled him in on the possibility of a production. The priest gladly agreed to play the part. He even said he would watch an old movie to make sure he also dressed the part. The professor then contacted the leader of the debate club that he had chosen for the ruse, Bradley Scott. He fully laid out the plan for Friday night, including that he did not know how many or if any would show up, but that they had to be prepared. Bradley had jumped to the challenge.

Friday came around all too soon. Ruth begged to come as the housekeeper to Sherlock and so he agreed if she wore a costume. Winston, Sir Wendel's son and a sophomore at Oxford, had also been told to connect with Bradley for his part to play. Wendel and Ruth arrived in style in their Mercedes and gathered early to prepare. The five students from Bradley Scott's 'Gulliver's Club' debate team also arrived with Winston close behind.

They discussed the debate topic: whether unconditional love can be found in the world. The two teams had their opening statements, proofs, and refutations ready. They took their seats and waited. Mr. Arbuckle was the first one to arrive. He probably came because he felt responsible. He tried to be pleasant. Then around twenty of the students showed up, and so did several parents. They were quietly shown their seats in a half circle around the tables set up theater style. The atmosphere was electric.

"Welcome to the 'love debate' as we are calling it. I welcome my close and dear friend, Dr. Watson."

The priest stood and made a short bow. The students were impressed.

"Now before we discuss this most important topic, I must lay down the rules of debate especially considering the subject matter: We never make fun of a person's looks or mock them in any way. We never make fun of someone's health or disability or use terms that try to point one's opinion toward a certain direction. Let your logic, ethics, and morals be the presenter of truth. Passion is fine, be sure it is passion of principle, not based on hatred or loathing. Passion should be based on justice. Always show respect for another's opinion. Do not disdain their views by expressing your disdain by your body language or facial expressions, et cetera. We do not use terms such as: stupid, ignorant, idiot, or foolish when referring to a person. The goal here is not an ambitious, self-exalting desire to win, or to feel good about one's debating skills. The desire is truth, and the attitude is humility. Answer all questions in the timeframe given. Would the teams line up at their tables, please?"

There were three on each team, five were from the original 'Gulliver's Club' then Winston made six. Dr. Watson was the mediator and the timekeeper. He began:

"First question, two minutes: can unselfish, unwavering love be found on this earth?"

Winston was first to speak, "We are defining this term 'love' using the Greek definition of 'agape' or a one-way love. This is the kind of love that reaches out to strangers to rescue them from danger or poverty. This is the kind of love that sent Jonathan Livingston to deepest Africa and in the end insisted that his heart be buried there. This is the kind of love that Corrie ten Boom had when she forgave the Nazi soldier who took part in the murder of her family.

"We can go through a list of people who have given their lives for the poor, hungry, sick, and disabled. This love heals, it does not kill, this love saves, it does not reject. I put forth this day that this love can only be found in God himself of whom it is said that He is love as stated in the book of First John, New Testament of the Bible."

"Time," piped up Mr. Watson. "One minute for cross-examination."

"Read that portion you failed to quote in your construct please," Bradley stifled a smile.

"Yes, that is from 1 John 4:8, 'Whoever does not love, does not know God, because God is love,'" replied Winston.

"Can you deduce the opposite from that statement, that whoever loves does know God?" inquired Bradley.

"Yes, the verse just before that one reads, 'Love is from God, and whoever loves has been born of God and knows God.'" Winston answered.

"Thank you, that is all," the negative team replied.

"Negative construct, two minutes. Begin." Dr. Watson nodded to the other team to proceed.

53

"We all know that there is a love on earth that is not connected to God. Every mother for her baby, for instance. Can you think of a mother on earth that would abandon her child? No, I say there is no God, and love is based on humanity being linked through first man and first woman. We are of one blood and that is what makes us loving. Other examples are a man's love toward his dog or devotion of a woman to a man. I believe that kind of love is everlasting and a bond that will never break. I have the authority of Plato himself that defined love as 'an intellectual conception' as stated in his symposium. If what you say is true then no atheist in the world would have the ability to love and by my experience of knowing quite a few non-religious people, I would say they are quite capable of love in the deepest of senses. How would we have populated the world so fully, progressed so completely if on a foundation of hatred, for isn't that the opposite of love?"

"Time, one minute to cross examine." Moderator Watson looked at his watch.

"Concerning your Plato reference, does he not say the highest elevation of love was a theological vision of love that transcends sensuality and mutual care?" the affirmative team asked.

"Yes, I believe so," was the reply.

"And isn't the definition of the opposite of love, indifference-a totally absence of care, not hatred?" the affirmative team continued.

"I am not aware of that definition." The negative team was not looking too good.

"No more questions." The affirmative team was finished.

"Affirmative team is up next, two minutes." Dr. Watson continued.

"You state that no mother on earth would abandon her baby. I would beg to differ. We hear of abandoned babies often. They are left in trash heaps across the globe. We have millions of proofs of this every day, every hour, every second with millions upon millions of mothers ending their pregnancies. Are they killing the most powerful love on earth? I don't think so. You speak of first man and first woman, sounds a bit like Adam and Eve, God's creation, created from dust for the purpose of a love relationship with Him. They walked with God every evening until they fell by listening to the greatest disturber of love, Satan.

"Yes, we are of one blood, but if this was truly our belief then there would be no more divisions or war. There is even war in families! And if what you say is true, then why is there divorce? Also, I wonder how long would it take for love to be lost between a master and his biting dog?"

The affirmative team had some worthy points.

"Time. Any cross-examinations?" Dr. Watson asked the negative team.

"No, sir."

"Negative concluding statement, two minutes, begin." Watson again looked at his watch.

"We know that there are mentally ill out there without the capability of love. They are the disturbers of love, not Satan. And of course, love must be conditional, why love a dog that bites? Get a new one. Why love a girl who cheats on you? Get a new one. Why even love a naughty, rebellious child? Love must be given in both directions. One who loves deserves to be loved in return. No one in his or her right mind would do otherwise. Why would missionaries or Corrie ten Boom or anyone else reach out to strangers, or forgive persecutors? Maybe they are the mentally ill because it makes no sense! Charles Darwin proved that we are no more than animals in a higher state of consciousness. We need to make an effort in society to work together enough to where we don't encroach on each other's space. That is all." It was a passionate presentation.

"Affirmative concluding statement, begin." The debate was winding down.

"What you are saying goes against what we believe at our deepest core, and I quote the greatest philosopher who has ever lived, 'Greater love has no man, than a man lay down his life for his friends'. Is this not the definition of love? The purpose of love, therefore, is giving. The result of love is joy and peace. The pursuit of love takes humility and hard work. And that, my friend does not come from the mentally ill!"

Sir Wendel, aka Sherlock Holmes, took the stand.

"We have run out of time ladies and gentlemen but thank you for attending." He stood near the door and handed each person his newly printed 'Sherlock Holmes' cards just in case they wanted to chat some more. Mr. Arbuckle was amused and thanked Sir Wendel for his time. He added that he thought it went quite well and if parents have a complaint, he will send them right over to see Dr. Sherlock Holmes.

CHAPTER 8

Deduction!

Ruth Salomon presented her husband with a small golden coin at the breakfast table.

"What is this?" he asked.

"I found it while on my morning walk. As I went through the park and passed a flowerbed, something reflecting the sun caught my eye. I think you might know its significance."

"Well, I do think you are right, my dear. It is a New Pence coin that was accidentally minted in 1983, worth about 650 pounds. We need to investigate this!" Sir Wendel finished his breakfast.

"Ruth, come and show me where you found that coin."

He put it into his pocket, wrapped a scarf around his neck, grabbed his umbrella and the couple headed toward the park.

"This is where I found it." Ruth explained, "Maybe it fell out of a hole in the gardener's pocket, or maybe in the dark, someone slipped it into his pocket and missed." She continued, "I guess it could have fallen out of a hot air balloon that was passing or a rat or dog may have carried it here!" Ruth was going over every possibility and smiling.

Sir Wendel walked around the flower patch then up a narrow path the gardener probably used. Frowning, he studied the ground and poked under the foliage.

"Ah, look here, Ruth. I found a footprint. It could be the gardeners."

Sir Wendel took out a piece of paper and traced, as well as he could, the print that was left in the damp soil.

"The shoe has a very distinctive and unusual squarish toe," noticed Ruth.

"I have a thought, Ruth, there is a coin collector down the street. I have driven by that shop. Let's walk over and see what he says."

The pair walked the eight blocks to the shop, which had a 'closed' sign posted, but they knocked anyway. A small, balding, and sad-looking man finally opened it a crack without removing the chain lock. "I'm sorry we are closed right now."

Sir Wendel held up the coin, "Does this happen to be yours?"

The door flew open, and the man snatched it up saying, "Where did you find this!"

The chain was removed then replaced and the three went into an office where Ruth relayed the morning's adventure.

"I was robbed last night!" the man moaned, "the police just left, but I have no confidence that they will help me recover what I have lost."

"We would like to try to help you if we can," offered Sir Wendel. "How many coins were stolen?"

"There were ten that were missing, now only nine thanks to you! I was just relieved that they didn't see the most expensive ones in the cabinet next to the ones that were taken. The added worth of my loss is about 2,000 pounds, but if the others had been taken, I would have been ruined!"

"Tell me about you and your family, Mr.....?

"My name is Saul Abrams. My wife Sarah and I have a son who is studying abroad. Don't ask me why. I also have a nephew, Luke, who lives with us and works part-time for me in the shop. I do not know what I would do without him. He keeps the place clean and tidy. We emigrated from Austria when the Nazis began their march across the land. We have lived here since that time and have had this shop for thirty years. I inherited a box of coins from my father and that is what we used to start the business. We sell other collectables, but the coins have the most value."

"Did the police find any clues when they came by? Did they offer any hope of retrieval?"

"No, I think they thought I had taken them to get insurance money. I didn't even tell them that I had no insurance on the coins. I was too angry! But I will tell you that I saw someone from my bedroom window run around the corner last night. It was 1:00 in the morning, but I had heard some noises, so I opened the window and looked out. I didn't know that I was being robbed!"

"Does your window make enough noise that he would have heard it being opened?" asked Sir Wendel.

"Very possible, since I rarely open it and it is rather sticky."

"Did you notice anything about his clothing?"

Mr. Abrams shook his head, "Just maybe a black hooded sweatshirt like the kids wear these days."

With words of encouragement, Sir Wendel excused himself and he and Ruth left the shop. The couple slowly walked back through the park and stood by the flowery mound.

"If you were a criminal, and you were nervous, thinking someone was chasing you, where would you go?" Sir Wendel asked Ruth. They stood and studied the landscape.

"I may think to run to the right, but the street is brighter that way as it has more lights. So, I may go left," decided Ruth.

"Or I may go straight ahead into that alley. It is the nearest and darkest place in which to hide for a few hours." Sir Wendel stated.

They walked toward the alley studying the ground as they went. The alley was the typical dark, dank, smelly, narrow passage that was only good for rubbish receptacles-thus the smell.

"I am going to look inside these trash cans. Ruth, you may want to step back." He pulled open the first one and poked around with his umbrella.

"We are going to have to get you a new one, Wendel."
Ruth had the nasal sound of one holding the nose between the
finger and thumb. Wendel moved on.

"Good thing the garbage men haven't come yet this
week. Good thing the people using these haven't used them yet
today, because, Voila! Look what I found!" Wendel was holding
a small leather drawstring pouch in his hand.

"That is only a child's marble bag, dear."

"Or maybe the thief had the coins in this, transferred
them into his pocket and then trashed the bag."

"Wendel, how can you be so certain?"

"Look, Ruth, this is a brand-new bag, it is even
expensive looking. Maybe it had been a gift, why else would he
want to be rid of it?"

Sir Wendel put the evidence into his pocket, which Ruth
did not appreciate, and he continued to open every bin. They
walked to the end of the row of bins and saw that the alley did
not have an exit. On turning around, Wendel spotted something
sticking out from behind the last rubbish can. He knelt and
pulled out a pair of black jeans and a hooded sweatshirt.

"Aha, here we are, the frightened young man came back
here, changed his clothes, and stuffed them here so that he could
get them later. He would have to come back in the next few days
before garbage day to retrieve them."

"Are we going to have a stake out, Wendel, and catch
him returning to the alley in the middle of the night?"

"We are getting too old for that, Dear. No, we will have
this solved before that!" he assured his wife as he went through
the pockets of the jeans. "Ah look, Ruth."

He held up a small piece of paper and read: "Tonight or
else!' Someone is being forced into a life of crime. Let's go back
to the shop, I have an idea."

Sir Wendel and his wife Ruth were again in the office of Mr. Abrams where Wendel laid out the clothing and the marble bag. "We found these in the alley about nine blocks from here. I am not saying that they are the criminal's belongings, but it is a possibility. Would you mind if I asked your nephew some questions about what he may have noticed yesterday. Maybe he has forgotten a detail."

While Saul went to find his nephew, Wendel whispered to Ruth, "I want to speak to the boy alone. Ask Mr. Abrams to show you something, anything from the shop."

Saul returned with a disheveled dark-headed boy in his early 20's. Sir Wendel met them at the door of the office and introduced himself to Luke as a professor at Oxford. Ruth took Mr. Abrams arm and asked if he would show her the women's gold watches. Wendel frowned.

Wendel went into the office first and turned in time to see Luke's face turn white.

"I found these clothes in an alley not far from here. I thought I would help your uncle with the burglary since my wife found one of the gold coins. Have a seat."

Sir Wendel took a glance at the boy's shoes then pulled out the tracing of the one from the park. Here is a footprint I found in the footpath where the coin was found. Looks like you have the same kind of shoe. May I see it?"

Luke mechanically slipped off his shoe and Wendel not only noticed that it was the exact same size, but there were bits of mud in the tread. He also pulled out the paper with the threatening words. Luke was no longer pale, but beet red with beads of sweat collecting on his forehead and upper lip.

"This is what I think happened. There is a boy who has been threatened by a gang of bullies and they possibly said they would kill a certain aunt and uncle if he didn't steal some treasures from the uncle's shop. The boy did break in but only took a small number of the coins in hopes that the crooks would be satisfied. The crooks were not, and the boy is being bullied to steal more. He is stuck. He can't turn them in because they know something about him that they are holding over his head."

Luke slid further down into his chair.

"I have a great plan that I think will work, if that boy agrees, and if it does work, the aunt and uncle need not know that it was he who took the coins."

Luke broke down and sobbed. Wendel quickly threw the discovered clothing onto the floor in front of the crack under the door so the weeping sound would not alert the uncle.

"Listen we haven't much time, you have to stop crying so I can tell you my plan. When are you meeting this gang and how many are there?" Wendel's whisper quieted Luke.

"I must meet them again tonight. There are ten that I know of." He wiped his eyes and blew his nose on the hanky Sir Wendel offered.

"What are they holding over you?"

"I played cards and lost, but I didn't really know how the game worked and I didn't know they were talking about money. They didn't give me a chance to turn them down. They also told me I had to get the money right then and took me to a house and had me break in and steal some jewelry. It was awful." Luke started crying again.

"SHH, okay, listen and do exactly what I say. I am sure they are having you followed so stay home. I am going to be back here in one hour with a ruse that I am talking to you about getting into Oxford."

"That's a good one!" Luke cynically mumbled.

"I will then let you know how we will handle tonight. Don't worry!" Wendel left with his wife who tried to get him to look at a watch she had found.

"We will be right back, Mr. Abrams. I want to show your nephew something that I think he is going to like!"

Sir Wendel relayed his plan to his wife as they walked home through the park. Several times he looked over his shoulder but wasn't too worried. Bad guys are rarely morning people. He called Scotland Yard and asked to be put through to Chief Inspector Newbury. He waited several minutes but finally the inspector answered and Wendel quickly related the story. The inspector was not happy as usual.

"Come in and meet with me, Sir Wendel. How about three this afternoon? If we are going to put this boy in danger, we had better do it right, with no mistakes!"

Wendel humbly agreed.

After hanging up, he grabbed a pile of college information and a box of gold coins. He left his wife at home and drove back to the shop. Mr. Abrams met him at the door and was much friendlier.

"Do you think you can talk the boy into college? I wish we had that kind of money around here." He hollered for Luke and then left them in the office.

"Luke, I want you to go to the meeting point tonight and carry these coins with you. In fact, maybe we should transfer them into your leather pouch. The gang gave it to you, right?"

"Yeah, how did you know?"

"Deduction. Anyway, when, and where are you meeting?" Urgency was in Sir Wendel's voice.

"Midnight, in the alley."

"When you hand over the money do you think they will leave you or take you with them?"

"They always just take what I give them. Hey, this is gold, and a lot of it! Is it yours?" Luke couldn't believe his eyes.

"I will not put more of your uncle's coins at risk, especially since we are trying to avoid him finding out. I think this is a good use of this money even if I do not get it back."

"Wow, I have never met anyone like you before. Who are you?"

"My name is Wendel Salomon. I am a professor at Oxford, currently on sabbatical. Now I must go!"

At three o'clock that afternoon in the St. James district of Westminster, Wendel knocked at the office of Chief Inspector Newbury.

"Come in!" the not-too-happy man bellowed, "Give me your plan and I will let you know if it is feasible."

Sir Wendel explained his proposal in detail and the only reaction he received was raised eyebrows when he said that he had given Luke twenty gold coins from his own collection.

"Was that necessary and wise? What if the kid skips town with your money?" the inspector rubbed his temples.

"At least he will be safe. That is what I care about. Also, I know you won't approve but I am going to try to keep Luke's involvement from his aunt and uncle and from the newspapers. He has been tortured enough and deserves a second chance."

"If this ends well and this gang is taken off the streets, then I will consider it."

"Thank you, sir." A grateful Sir Wendel made his exit.

At eleven that night, officers hid in trees, in unmarked cars, and in the park with binoculars. Sir Wendel sat with the chief inspector down the street, and both were watching like hawks. They saw Luke enter the alleyway.

"I guess he didn't skip town. DUCK!"

The men slouched down in the car as a black Nissan slowly drove by. They watched as Luke stepped out of the darkness and handed them the bag. Instead of just taking the bag they shoved him into the car. The chief immediately grabbed his walkie-talkie and told everyone to stand down.

"We are going to plan B. We will follow far behind them. I will be first. Call in the license plate, Sarge. Follow two blocks behind us. Let's move!"

Wendel had really hoped and prayed that it would not go like this. They had planned to follow the car, but not with Luke in it.

"God, help tonight go well!" he said aloud. The inspector ignored him. He was angry.

The car followed far behind the Nissan and Wendel kept binoculars on the target. The streets were fairly empty and if they had gotten too close things could go wrong, terribly wrong.

"They turned left at the next light!" noted Sir Wendel.

They ran the red light and slowed to a crawl. The street was dark. The chief shut off the headlights and crept along. They looked down every driveway, alley, and into every parking lot.

"God give us a clue!" whispered Sir Wendel. They drove a few more blocks, and to their left stood an old warehouse, Sir Wendel saw a light flicker then go off.

"That's it!" cried Wendel. The chief inspector jumped out of his skin.

They parked the car on the street, and the call was made to all the trailing police cars. Soon the building was surrounded. Wendel followed the inspector through the unlocked door and Wendel pointed up, so they went up the steps. Soon loud muffled voices came from an office and then a yell. Wendel prayed. The inspector motioned the team to follow him up the stairs. All ten officers held guns and the chief slipped one to Wendel but motioned to him to stand way back. He counted to three by holding up fingers, one, two, three, and the officers burst into the room yelling and screaming, "GET DOWN, HANDS WHERE I CAN SEE THEM!"

The chief yelled again and that got them moving. Handcuffs were applied, Luke was untied, and Wendel led him off.

"Luke, where do they keep their stash?" Wendel didn't want to sound too anxious about getting his bag of gold back.

"I'll show you." They went down into the warehouse and Luke opened one of a line of cupboards. The first one had no lock, and it held the bag of gold.

"May I take this, sir?" he asked the chief who had joined them.

"No, this is evidence... never mind." He saw the loot and decided that Wendel's bag wasn't needed. "I think we will find your uncle's coins here too. Goodnight and thank you for your help, Son. I hope you are okay?"

"Yes, sir, and thank you for saving me!"

An officer drove them both home and after promising to meet the next day, Luke sneaked back into his bedroom.

Ruth was sitting up and waiting for her husband to get home. She had prayed the entire day and was so relieved that the ordeal was over. Wendel filled her in on a few details then shut off the lights.

The next day Sir Wendel visited Mr. Abrams one last time and told him that the police had caught the gang red-handed and that he would be getting his coins back after the trial.

"May I take Luke out for lunch? I think I may have some good news for him about his future at Oxford. You wouldn't mind if he was able to attend would you, Mr. Abrams?"

"It would be my deepest wish come true!" he replied.

Over lunch Sir Wendel explained there had been a reward for helping with the capture of this gang and that Luke would receive it. He also explained that Luke should tell his uncle the whole story. He then explained that he wanted to tutor

Luke to help him get into Oxford. He would administer a test to see what areas of study that they could work on together.

"Would you like this, Luke?"

"I have always wanted to be a scientist, Professor. I just never thought it a possibility." His eyes were filling up, "I have something to show you, sir." Luke lifted his shirtsleeve. There was a large X on his upper arm.

"I don't think the university would let me in with this. The gang did this the first night I lost the card game. It is their symbol." Luke dropped his sleeve and looked down at his half-eaten sandwich.

"Why, Luke, that looks exactly like the Greek letter Chi, or the first letter of the name Christ, referring of course to Jesus. Let's say that you now belong to Jesus. That He has your future in His hands and that your life is now going to be a life of advancement!"

"I would like that, but I'm Jewish!"

"So is He!" Sir Wendel told him the story of Jesus and why He came as the Jewish Messiah to save all the earth.

Luke prayed to receive Christ as his Lord.

"The purpose of education, Luke, is to serve others and God. The goal is never to be better than others, or to feel pride in your position. I think you will serve well!"

That night over dinner, Wendel and Ruth discussed the excitement of the week.

"We should never give into fear when fighting for someone's life." Sir Wendel pondered.

"And we should never put money before people," remarked his wife as she admired her new gold watch.

CHAPTER 9

⇔

The Great Divide

Sir Wendel Salomon was minding his own business, standing on the street corner, waiting to cross, when two men flew out of the local pub right in front of him. The larger fellow punched the other's nose so hard that Wendel was certain he heard a crack.

Time seemed to stand still from that point on. The police, ambulance, and the crowd all gathered. Statements were taken and Wendel went home with a troubled heart. Three months passed and the police, the crowd and Sir Wendel again gathered, this time in the courtroom. The hearing went quickly because the defendant, Roderick Roberts, a chagrined fellow with a hangdog look, pled guilty to punching Fred Bowles in the face, breaking his nose, and nearly doing him in. No jury needed, no lawyers butting in to muddy the waters, only Judge Jennifer Winter was there, delivering the verdict and sentencing the guilty man.

"Five years at the HMP Pentonville prison, this is your third offence and I do not want to see you in this courtroom ever again!" The gavel gave its historic 'whack.'

"All rise," the court bailiff called out as the judge left her seat.

"Court dismissed," he added after she had exited the room.

The crowd dissipated and Sir Wendel went home. He immediately called the prison to make an appointment to visit the prisoner, Roderick Roberts; the appointment was in three weeks. Sir Wendel would have preferred not to make the long trip to the unhappy institution of confinement, but his mission was clear.

Mr. Roberts walked into the meeting room, head down and looking rather pathetic in his drab jumpsuit. He took a seat facing Sir Wendel.

"Do you remember me, Roderick?" asked Sir Wendel, "I witnessed your altercation and came to the trial."

Roderick kept silent.

"I think I can help you be free. Do you want to listen to what I have to offer?"

Roderick raised his eyes and replied, "Are you a lawyer?"

"No, but I have taught a few. I am offering my services for free, and I have excellent references."

"Why would you want to waste your time on me?" mumbled Roderick.

"That I will speak of later. But for now, let me know your decision."

"There is no decision," the prisoner emphatically and angrily assured the professor, "I'm in, what choice do I have?" Roderick's voice held despair and hopelessness.

"OK, good. My proposition is from a Bible verse that says: 'For the word of God is alive and active. Sharper than any double-edged sword, it penetrates even to the dividing of soul and spirit, joints and marrow; it judges the thoughts and attitudes of the heart.'"

Roderick frowned.

"Hear me out. Tell me what links you to that uncontrollable rage? Where did it come from? Think back through your past to where you first remember it."

"Well, my dad was worse than I am. He had real raging anger and violence, for no reason. When my mom was angry with me, she would say that I was just like him."

"There it is, a lie connecting the judgment you had against your father and the one your mother had against you. It went down into your soul and hid between it and your spirit. It hid there until anger released that lie and it became a reality. The truth is the sword of God's Word, and the truth about anger is that the anger of man does not accomplish the righteousness of God. The truth is that you have inherited certain genetic qualities from your father, but this thing is not one of them and it must go! Do you remember anything else?"

"When I was in fifth grade some boys made fun of me in school. I was so angry that I spent the whole rest of that year secretly getting even: tacks on their seats, glue on their notebooks, and such. They knew it was me but couldn't catch me."

"Another important memory," interjected Sir Wendel, "the truth is that vengeance is God's, not ours. If everyone spent their lives doling out punishment, everyone would be a punisher and everyone would be punished. Saying that God should stop all the bad or evil things in the world from happening has the same basic premise. God allows us to be bad, and God and he alone will someday punish the badness of the world. If everyone took vengeance, the result would be a society of anarchy and chaos. If God stopped the bad things, we would hate him for restraining us. The result would be an inner rebellion or a robotic science fiction novel. Can you imagine God grabbing your arm as you started to punch that man Fred in the nose?"

"Wish He would have," was Roderick's sad reply.

"But what if you were going to drink too much alcohol thereby becoming a danger to self and others? What if every time anyone broke the law they would be caught and made to pay a fine or be put in jail. What if God locked up every person on earth as soon as they became corrupt or cheated on their taxes or mistreated someone? There would be no room in the jails and the jailers would be incarcerated also! Can't you see? People want God to stop natural disasters, but they do not want him to stop their own personal disasters."

"I think so, but what do I do?" Roderick asked.

"You cannot keep yourself from evil, nor can you be trusted to judge others correctly. So, the answer is giving your life to the one true God who offered his son's life for yours. Not just to forgive you of your sins and faults but also to remove the lies hidden between your soul and your spirit and give you power to overcome sin. Will you join me in prayer?"

The convinced man glanced at the guard and decided it was worth the embarrassment.

"Good, pray and ask for forgiveness."

Roderick awkwardly did so. Sir Wendel cued him in to repent, to forgive his father and mother and release them from his judgments and put them into God's hands. He also forgave the boys who bullied him in school, and forgave himself for his rage.

Sir Wendel prayed next, "I expose the lies that have controlled Roderick all his life. I break off the words 'you are just like your father' over him and remove those fiery darts of the evil one. I declare the truth that vengeance is God's; Roderick has repented of taking vengeance himself and he is forgiven. Anger and rage no longer have its grip on Roderick; he chooses to be a forgiving person able to fully control himself."

Sir Wendel's time was up. "I left some notes and a Bible for you. I'll come back as soon as I can."

Wendel rose and left the room and Roderick, feeling much lighter and having a bit of hope again, wondered how Wendel was going to get him set free.

In the months to come, Sir Wendel was faithful to visit and pray with Roderick. Slowly his old, sinking posture turned to a straight, confident one. He treasured the time he had with his new mentor and friend. He even forgot the initial 'freedom' conversation and when he did, he came to realize his freedom had come from inside himself. Leading Bible studies, sharing his testimony, and encouraging the hopeless, became his favorite pastimes.

Walking outside after one of his prison visits, Sir Wendel ran into an old friend, "What are you doing here, Paul?"

"I was just hired as a part-time psychiatrist slash counselor here at the prison. It is nice to finally get to use my college degree. I think it will turn into a full-time position, as those men in there need lots of positive input!"

"I hate to say this, Paul, but you don't look well."

"I know, Wendel, I haven't slept in weeks. I'm nervous and worried about this new job. It is getting worse. I am starting to fret about driving and falling asleep at the wheel!"

"My frayed friend, God gives his beloved sleep! Are you God's beloved, Paul?"

"Nah, don't think so."

"It's time to become one. No better time than when one is in desperate need."

"OK, yes, I am terribly desperate, what do I do?"

"Prayer, praise, and petition. Tell you what, I'll buy you coffee when you are finished here." Sir Wendel offered.

"I just have to turn in these papers, and I will be right out. There is a coffee shop right down the road." Wendel's friend replied.

"Prayer is the first step," continued Sir Wendel after they were seated and had ordered. "But," he added, "You start the prayer with making the relationship right between you and God. Since He cannot look at sin, you first repent. Because Jesus paid for your freedom through his death on the cross, all you need to do is accept Him and submit to the life, the abundant life, which he is offering you."

Sir Wendel at that point folded his hands, bowed his head, and closed his eyes. His friend felt embarrassed but got the message.

"God, forgive me for living for myself and for not giving you the time of day. I am sorry for my sins, and I accept your sacrifice and I want the life you have for me."

Sir Wendel opened his eyes and encouraged Paul to pray for his sleep problems. He simply asked for God to help him sleep.

"Now the next step is to thank God!" So, they both thanked God and paused to receive their tea and sandwiches.

"Now, let's petition God for your new job. Lord, help my friend Paul to have much wisdom, peace, and influence in his work at the prison."

"So, we prayed, praised, and petitioned. There is one more thing and it is one of the Ten Commandments. You need to take a Sabbath day of rest. It is important to take at least one day a week to build relationships with God and with your family. You are to stop your regular work and enjoy the day. Trust in God, Paul. Rely on Him!"

After they had finished and were parting ways, Sir Wendel gave Paul a Bible (he kept a pile of them in his trunk).

"Start with 1 John, it is where I inserted some notes. My number is there too, call me anytime."

"Thank you, my friend!"

Within the week, Paul had called Sir Wendel to tell him that he was sleeping like a baby and enjoying his job. He told about meeting a great kid named Roderick and how they study together and engage the men in discussions.

"My wife and children seem happier also. I go with them to church, and we have been having picnics, playing card games together, and taking day trips when we can.

Thank you again, Sir Wendel!" Wendel hung up and picked up a small piece of paper with an address on it.

"Time to go and see how a Mr. Fred Bowles is doing."

CHAPTER 10

The Truth Revealed

Sir Wendel Salomon felt ready to tackle the world. He had spent a week in research and was anxious to crack the Siberian mystery. He was making a list of items to bring on his long-anticipated journey when the phone rang.

"Sir Wendel, I am calling for the Baroness Amelia Crawford. I think you would remember her as the one who gave a rather large donation to the Logic Society at Oxford?"

"Yes, of course, I remember her well. Is everything alright?"

"No. This is Alice, her maid, and I have been instructed to urgently request your presence at Crawford Hall. Her ladyship has some important information to relay." The maid was clearly reading off a dictated note.

"Ma'am, I will be right over. It will take me approximately thirty minutes depending on traffic." Sir Wendel conveyed the information to his wife who helped him pick out a tie. He left looking rather spiffy with his neck wrapped in a silk scarf and his brand-new umbrella under his arm.

The valet parked his car and was greeted by a tall, stiff butler.

"This way, Sir." Wendel was led up three flights of stairs, down a hall and into a pink bedroom.

"Hello, madam, I hear that you have requested to see me?"

"Oh, Wendel, so glad you have come." Lady Crawford motioned for her nurse, maid, and butler to all leave the room.

"Do you remember me?" the elderly lady's voice was just above a whisper.

"Of course, Milady, yours has been the largest donation in the history of the Logic Society (he did not mention that it was the only one). But I remember you not just for your kindness and generosity, but also for the lively conversation we had at the orphanage fundraiser. Do you remember that?" She blinked and weakly smiled.

"I don't have much time or energy, so listen carefully. There is a pad and a pen beside my bed. I want you to write down exactly what I dictate to you. Hurry now." Wendel grabbed the items and readied himself for the dictation.

"To whom it may concern: On this day of November 28, 1988, I, Countess Amelia Crawford with a sound mind do call null and void all former wills and do now bequeath all of my worldly possessions to Sir Wendel Salomon, professor at Oxford University, head of the Logic Department." She then reached for the pen and paper and signed and dated it in her own hand.

"Thank you, Wendel. I am sorry that you are going to be involved in a fight with my four children. But never fear, you will bring peace to the war that is coming. Water please."

He gave her a sip of water and she motioned for him to ring the bell. He did so and the maid and nurse entered. She motioned for them to come close.

"I am in my right mind, Alice and Nurse Rodgers. I have just had Sir Wendel aid me in rewriting my will. Please look at it and attest that this is my handwriting." They did. "Now leave me," she ordered them.

"Your children have arrived, ma'am," the nurse interjected.

"Give me ten minutes, then send them in," the dying heiress instructed.

Wendel had to bend his ear toward her mouth, as she began to tell him about her children.

"Wallace is 65, an honorable member of parliament, has an estranged wife, three grown children and is in more debt than he can possibly pay off on his own. Then there is Estelle, age 60, a clothes designer, well known, but lives above her means and is in more debt than she can possibly pay off on her own. Then there is Gilbert, age 57, Doctor of Optometry, wife and two children and in more debt than he can pay off on his own. And lastly, George, 55, a professional gambler and terrible with relationships and is in more debt than he can pay off on his own.

"Do you get the picture, Sir Wendel? You can see they want me dead, and they want my money. Now I know that when people get old, they sometimes become senile and paranoid. I am neither! I want you to determine whether I have made the right decision."

The countess' voice was fading. Sir Wendel gave her another sip of water and she whispered, "Go to my lawyer now." She pointed to a card on her nightstand. Sir Wendel took the card and the will, kissed her hand and at the same moment the four adult children entered the room. He nodded to them then departed.

Sir Wendel followed the address to a brownstone building on High Street and made himself known to the clerk. He waited for half an hour before a young man appeared and showed him into a spacious room with a high ceiling.

"Presenting Sir Wendel Salomon, Sir."

He was ushered to a seat and was greeted warmly by a rather plump and polite lawyer.

"Hello, my name is Rogers, Samuel Rogers, how can I help you?"

"I am here on behalf of the Countess Amelia Crawford. We have been acquainted for some time now and I have won her trust and confidence. I am a Professor of Logic at the University of Oxford, and it is through that venue that we have come to know each other. This morning she rang me up to have me write another will for her, which I now present to you. It was also acknowledged by her maid and her nurse before I brought it here."

The man donned his spectacles and read the missive.

"You know that the four will certainly take this to court," smiled the lawyer. "I am sorry that I find this rather humorous, because it really isn't... just a minute."

He rang for his assistant and requested that he retrieve the Crawford will, the Countess Amelia's. Soon the man brought in the document, but before he could reveal its contents the four Crawford descendants burst into the room.

"I am sorry, sir, I couldn't stop them!" the concerned assistant announced.

"It is fine, Smith, bring in extra chairs." The rotund lawyer leaned back into his and soon bade the group to have a seat.

"Tell me, gentlemen and ma'am, why have you burst in on us in such a manner?"

"Our dear mother has just passed away and this man has had her rewrite her will, as our maid, Alice, has told us." They glared at Sir Wendel. "We demand to hear what she has written!"

The lawyer, trying not to show his true feelings, read what Sir Wendel had given him. The four of them ranted and raved until the lawyer could take it no more.

"Quiet! I will now read the will which you may certainly go to court to attempt to have reenacted."

He proceeded to read, "The Van Gogh painting of the sunflowers was to go to the Museum of Art in London. The Estate itself would go to The Holy Apostles Catholic Church for the explicit purpose of an orphanage. The crystal necklace will go to Estelle, the gun collection to Wallace, the coin collection to Gilbert and the silver set to George. The rest to be donated to the Salvation Army on Dundas Street, London."

The entire clan was pale and silent. They did not move a muscle as they saw their entire fortune and salvation slip away. It was as if the air had been kicked out of them. The lawyer and Sir Wendel both rose at the same time and slipped out the door.

"Best give them some time to digest this shocking news," smiled Samuel Rogers, "but come here." They walked over to the man's desk, and he turned on an intercom in time to hear the four slowly come to their senses.

"Don't think she liked us much. I thought that necklace was diamonds," said the monotone voice of Estelle.

"I guess hoping for her death wasn't really the answer to our problems was it!" One of them angrily revealed.

"Guess we should go; we will let that professor handle everything and we can get on with our pathetic lives." It was clear they were getting up to leave. The intercom was shut off and Sir Wendel had an idea.

"I have a plan, Mr. Rogers, in spite of the greed of these people, I have to believe that an inheritance will help improve the lives of this family." They both walked back into the room.

"People, please sit down. I am willing to give up the will that I received this morning if you prefer."

They shook their heads, "We don't care what you do." Estelle answered.

"Is there anything of your mother's that you would like to own, the coins, the necklace, the guns or the silver?"

"No, I think we would just sell them anyway. We aren't really into that stuff." George mumbled.

"I am not really into stuff either," continued Wendel. "And I am sure you do not want to live in the mansion?"

They shook their heads.

"How much money do you each need to get you out of debt and get you on your feet again?" Despite the intrusive question, they all answered. The amounts ranged from 30,000 to 50,000 pounds.

"Have hope and give me all your phone numbers. I will get back to you. Here is my phone number in case you think of anything you would want from the estate." They exchanged numbers and the foursome left, looking a little less depressed.

The next day, Wendel went to the Holy Apostles Catholic Church and talked to the priest about whether he needed a home for orphans. He responded with a thank you, but no. Then Wendel went to an acquaintance, a Mr. Levi Lerner, who owned an auction house. The date was set up for the estate auction in two months' time.

"We take 30% of the money from the auction, or 20% if you donate to us all of the remaining goods that does not sell," the proprietor proposed.

Sir Wendel agreed to the 20%, and they set a time to meet at the estate to begin marking everything for auction. It took several weeks, even with a team of twelve employees.

Mr. Lerner then notified Sir Wendel, "Well, sir, we have gone through everything and the estimated worth, excluding the mansion and the Van Gogh, is 2 million pounds. And I was wondering if you would consider selling me the castle? I had an informal estimate done by a friend of mine, and it is way over what I can afford, but I would like to make an offer of 7 million pounds. I could move my office and display space to the entire main floor." The man was clearly excited about the idea.

"Sold!" Sir Wendel was as thrilled as the auctioneer. The auction was a success, nearly everything sold. Wendel first made a trip to the Catholic Church and donated the 7 million pounds in fulfillment of the countess' wish. He then called the four siblings and met them at the same lawyer's office where they had first gathered. Sir Wendel handed them each a check for 300,000 pounds. The thankful, humbled, and relieved Crawford siblings walked out with smiles on their faces. With the issue solved and the weight of burden removed, Wendel headed home. He walked into his house heading straight for his office, sat down, and looked up at a beautiful painting of sunflowers hanging on his   wall.

CHAPTER 11

One Last Opportunity

A knock on the front door was a rare occurrence for the Salomon household. A professor's address is not easily retrieved for reasons of safety and privacy. But a knock could be the postman with a package from relatives in Estonia, or someone lost in the neighborhood, which has happened, or a surprise visit from Winston, but being the last week of his junior year at Oxford, it seemed unlikely. Sir Wendel made his way to see who it was at the door.

"Finn! Good to see you. Come in!" Finnegan O'Hara was an old professor friend. In fact, he had the distinction of being the oldest among the group of professors at Oxford.

"I haven't seen you in ages! How are you?"

"Having a struggle with arthritis." Finnegan showed Wendel his hands. The joints of his fingers were swollen, crooked, and stiff looking.

"I can't write or type any longer, so I'm relieved that it is the end of the year. That is why I dropped by. A specialist in Liverpool can see me on Monday. Now I know I could cancel my remaining class, but I just have a hard time doing it. I have given the final already, everything is finished, but if you could do me a favor and lecture on Monday at one in the afternoon to wrap things up?"

"Sure, Finn, are you still teaching World Religions?" Wendel asked.

"Yes, that would be it. Also, I have asked a student, Geoff Franks, if he would tape the session for me, if you don't mind." Sir Wendel agreed, and they parted ways without shaking hands. He felt dreadfully sorry for his old friend.

Sir Wendel spent much time in prayer and study as he knew this was an important in-road to the hearts of these Oxford students and could be their only time to hear the truth from a Biblical worldview.

"Good afternoon, students, I am Professor Salomon, substitute for your final World Religions class. Congratulations on finishing the year and I trust that you have finished strong. We are going to summarize in this last hour, and hopefully make some final suppositions on what we have learned this year. I am also trusting that I can learn something from you also. I never did have the pleasure of taking this particular class when I was a student. So feel free to give input on the topics we will discuss today. Mr. Franks have you begun the recording?"

"Yes, sir." Sir Wendel thanked him and scanned the large theater style, wood paneled room. He looked into the uninterested eyes of the 75 juniors who yearned to be beginning their summer break. He began.

"My question today is one that I have pondered for many years now, and I would be obliged if you could help answer it. I have traveled to several countries that hold to specific religions and I have noticed that I have never seen, nor have I read about a protest march against any of these belief systems, unless you think communism is a religion. Now I do know that each belief system has strict rules for living. Most have very strict laws for women to follow. They have harsh and sometimes cruel judgments for the breaking of these laws, and yet no one ever raises a fist at any one of their gods. But, in the Christian Western world, people raise their fists all the time in defiance and rebellion toward the Christian God or at least against His standards."

Sir Wendel paused before continuing, "The Judeo-Christian God is merciful, kind, and promises hope for those who would submit to Him and follow His ways." Sir Wendel drew a large circle on the whiteboard.

"This can be illustrated by this circle labeled 'Trust in God.' The basic principle here is that if you stay inside of this circle of compliance, then you will be protected and blessed. Why would someone not want that? The problem as I see it, is that God is seen as a killjoy, an all-powerful One who does not allow us to have any fun. It seems obvious to me that after the external so-called pleasures are over, those outside the circle are not the joyous, happy folks that they claim to be. They seem to need those pleasure crutches to keep life from being depressing. Addictions are common today but what addiction has ever given someone a fulfilled life?" Sir Wendel wrote on the board outside of his circle the different kinds of addictions. He added rebellion.

"Rebellion is an addiction. It is a powerful feeling that makes one feel smarter and wiser than one's authority figures, whether parents, bosses, church or government. I happen to think that rebellion is what usually keeps us on the outside of this circle.

"Let's look at the Israelites after leaving Egypt. They were rescued over and over again but could never trust God enough to ask Him to help in time of their need, instead they chose to grumble against Moses. Moses was on a mountain for forty days to meet with God and to receive the Ten Commandments on tablets. During that time the people made an Egyptian idol and worshiped it. This was the same Egyptian religion that not only held them in bondage, but also killed their children by dumping them into the river Nile. Is that the answer, that people do not want to serve the good, and that they want to serve the painful, the cruel, and the false? Any thoughts?"

Sir Wendel waited a long time to allow the students to reply.

Finally, one man replied, "We do like to do what we want, when we want, but that does not explain why we need religion. Why does every people group have some type of worship to some type of god?"

"Anyone want to respond?" Sir Wendel paused briefly then continued, "Lenin implemented the communist manifesto and, in the process, massacred millions of his own people. He would not allow worship of any kind saying that religion 'is an opiate for the people', and yet for decades multitudes of Russian people have lined up to see his well-preserved corpse. And the purpose of this processional? Worship. He controlled, impoverished, and enslaved his own people, and on his deathbed allegedly declared that he had been wrong, that the purpose of his reign was to bring freedom and yet it brought only evil and massacre. Why indeed is there something within us that desires to worship? Could it be that God created us with that need so we would seek Him?"

"Much religion is about power and control. Those at the top demand to be worshiped and if they aren't, then there is retaliation," a girl in the second row tersely remarked.

Sir Wendel continued, "Is worship the same thing as fear? Maybe we worship what we fear? Let us define terms. Webster says that worship is reverence, respect, admiration, and devotion to an object of esteem. We desire to esteem something higher and better than ourselves. I think that Lenin was a poor choice. Fear can also have that meaning, but it also describes the anxious feeling when one is threatened and endangered. I think that is why we cower to bullies. They make us want to cave into their demands.

"Let's discuss something else, the problem of pain and suffering. What is the response of people whether inside or outside of the circle when they begin to experience life's painful circumstances? Some people respond by shaking their fist at God. Their belief that an all-powerful God should banish all suffering is a modern-day belief. My opinion, and you can tell me what you think, is that pain should bring us to our knees in front of the Almighty, pleading for His mercy and healing. Charles Darwin lost his daughter, and some believe that was what caused the rift between him and God. Let us say for discussion that this is true, that he decided he couldn't serve a God who 'took' his child. The problem is viewpoint. They could have been together for eternity. I think impatience is the opposite of faith. Any thoughts?"

The room was silent.

"Let's look at the self-proclaimed atheist. He believes that life is a random series of good and evil, based on nothing more than accidents and fate. He shakes his fist at Heaven, even when he does not believe anyone is up there. The problem with pain, is that even atheists want someone to blame, so they blame the people who believe in a gracious God, hate them in fact. This is like Marx's hatred for anyone who believed anything. Who is there to be angry with if pain is random?"

"Maybe when God allows evil things to happen, people think that He could have prevented it if he had wanted to, so they develop a belief that God is unloving," a man in the third row suggested.

"Good point. Let's consider this. If people would read the
Bible, which has the ultimate description of God, His personality, His desires, and His opinions, one would notice in Genesis chapter 6 that just before the flood that destroyed all but eight people, God's heart was full of pain because of all the

86

violence and wickedness that was going on in the earth. His purpose in sending the flood was to end the misery. Children were being tortured and sacrificed and God did do something about it. That isn't to say that every disaster is from the hand of God. When man failed to keep the one and only command given in the Garden of Eden, he handed dominion of the earth to God's greatest adversary, the devil.

"Job, who lived thousands of years ago, suffered unimaginable loss: his wealth, his ten children and his health, yet he refused the advice of his wife which was to curse God and die. He chose to stay inside of that circle by hanging on to his belief in the God of love. God showed up, and Job, amazed by God's power and awesomeness, repented for his finite ideas and his short-sighted views of the Almighty. God then doubled the blessing of Job."

"What religion was Job?" loudly piped up a man in the back row.

"Religion, defined by the original Latin, is a binding obligation in life. The book of James says it is taking care of widows and orphans and keeping one-self unpolluted morally. Let's just say Job was a God-fearing man who did his religious duty. Saying one is a Christian just because he is born into a Christian home or attends a church is not what Job's religion was about. He not only knew about God, but also wanted to honor Him. At the end of Job's trial, God spoke, and we can all learn more about God from Job's experience. Our seeking for truth will hopefully lead us to the same end. We need to know God.

"So really, the question is, do we want to willingly give our life to the one true God and enter the promises he has given us, or do we want to live outside of his will and take our chances? And I am not suggesting that living inside God's protective circle is a bed of roses, I am only suggesting that in the living we would never be alone. God's heart was in pain before the flood because he wanted a family. God wants a relationship with His creation, and He wants to bless his people, but they chose, and we choose a counterfeit to the good that God provides. He still does and that is why he sent Jesus, His son, to pay for our sins and bring us back into that relationship that humanity lost in the Garden of Eden. No other religion is based on relationship with its god. Don't you agree that when it comes down to it, love and forgiveness are key to that relationship? He forgives us if we ask, and we need to forgive too. If you must, pick the 'religion' that will fill you with love. There is only one that I can think of. Any remarks?

"I would like to present another thought." Sir Wendel continued after pausing, "The God of the Bible is known to be all powerful, all knowing, and everywhere present. This causes people to assume that he is a Mr. Fix-it or Santa that never gives out coal. Scripture says that all things are laid bare and are open before him. But it also says that the eyes of the Lord move throughout the earth to strengthen those whose hearts are fully committed to Him. My point is, God pays attention to those who are His, but if you ignore God, you cannot be angry when He ignores you in your time of disaster. But 'Whoever calls on the Lord will be saved.' He has open arms to those who call out to Him. He also says, 'Call to me and I will answer you. I will show you great and hidden things which you do not know.'"

"Professor, are you trying to get us to become Christians?" a back row man asked.

"Yes, sir, I am. I have been a Professor of Logic for many years. I have studied the philosophers and their contradictions. I have made a very logical choice to believe the truth of the Bible. This is not to say that faith was not needed, because any belief system takes faith. I can say with confidence that I have made the right choice and the joy, peace, and harmony with my creator has been the result."

"Aren't you breaking college rules by talking like this?"

"I am not sure of the rules that you speak of. This is a class on religion is it not? I talk about what I know. I also know that if I am wrong, who cares? We all die and will be no more. If I am right, then whoever of you rejects this message will forever be separated from a loving and kind creator for an eternity in a place that is not Heaven."

"A little harsh, don't you think, Professor?" a voice from the back insisted.

"Not really, we are given a choice just like Adam and Eve had a choice in the garden. I can see no reason not to choose the good path, unless one wants to do what one wants to do no matter how vile or wicked. Sir, what is harsh about that?"

"Just because I choose my own life in my own way, should not mean I am destined for hell!" came the same agitated voice.

"Answer this, sir, just because you choose to break the Ten Commandments and hurt others by what you do, should you be given a free get-out-of-jail pass? Inside of everyone is a desire for justice and because God is a just God, evil and wicked men must be punished."

"Yes, but I am not evil or wicked!" the same man getting even more angry replied.

"Hmm, then to prove my point, I would like you to list your sins right now and allow the class to decide. Have you ever stolen something that wasn't yours? Have you ever hurt a person or animal? Have you lied or been rude to your parents? Have you devalued someone by taking advantage of them?" Sir Wendel paused between each question and knowingly made the class very uncomfortable.

"There is not one person in here that does not deserve retribution for an action, including me. There are those in this room, including me, who have chosen to ask God for forgiveness, who have become free from the guilt and shame of their sin and who have given their lives over to the loving hands of our creator. He has a purpose for each, and this destiny is a very satisfying one. You may graduate and enter your career of choice, but you may be forever disappointed with your choice. Only God knows what will truly bring you joy. And only God can remove your pain. King Asa, as recorded in II Chronicles 16, died with a foot disease because he would not ask God for healing. Is that fair? All he would have had to do was ask. You tell me, was he required to do something difficult or painful? No, all he had to do was ask. What keeps us from asking?"

"Pride." someone shouted.

"I would have to agree. It takes a bending of the knee, of submitting one's ways to God's ways, and scripture declares that every knee will bow to Jesus Christ. If you do it now, you avoid an eternity of regret."

The angry man moved further down in his seat; three girls in the room were nodding their heads at him, and he was feeling the glare of their stares. They clearly had something against the fellow.

"I will end with this, if you want Christ, and forgiveness, repent and ask him to take over your life. Submit to Him. If not, go on with your future and have a good time, hopefully not at the expense of someone else's." He added, "If you have further questions, you may pick up one of my cards that I will leave on the table." Sir Wendel left the room.

Three weeks later, Sir Wendel received a phone call from Professor O'Hara.

"Hello Finn. I hope you are feeling better, and the treatments are working?" Sir Wendel was preparing for a barrage of rebuke concerning the class he taught and the subsequent recording the professor had surely listened to.

"The treatments were bogus, but yours wasn't! I listened to what you had to say, and I believe you are right. I asked God to heal me, and my hands are improving. Wendel, you were right. Thank you and I promise to play that recording every day of religion class from now on. God bless you, my friend!"

CHAPTER 12

The Conspiracy

The large box being carried into the home of Sir Wendel Salomon contained something that he had never purchased before. In a startling change of opinion, Sir Wendel purchased a television set.

"Dear," he had said earlier that day, "I think we need to keep up on what is happening in the world. I want to do my part to be informed." She hadn't known what he meant by that at the time.

Two hours later, after Sir Wendel had unboxed, unwrapped, and plugged in a 32-inch TV set and had arranged the antenna; he was soon watching his first news report.

"Ruth, would you bring me some biscuits and tea, please?" he bellowed.

"So, it has begun," she thought to herself.

After an hour of numerous commercials, the Oxford professor was ready to turn it off when he heard a shocking announcement.

"Oxford University's Vice-Chancellor, Dr. Morgan Westcott, is being accused of lining his pockets with school funds. His mansion, multiple motor vehicles, his luxurious living, and traveling had put him on very serious notice with the tax commission and the College Board. We will be reporting on this in the next few days, and we will keep you posted."

Sir Wendel was beside himself in disbelief. "This cannot be, can it?" he asked himself. Reaching for his phone, he called his friend and mentor, Dr. Westcott, but couldn't reach him.

Sir Wendel grabbed his jacket and flew out of the house, even forgetting his scarf and umbrella. "Don't wait up for me, Dear," he added as he exited.

Soon he was at the Vice-Chancellor's office and the secretary insisted that her boss was not seeing anyone.

"He will see me, I assure you. Tell him that Sir Wendel Salomon is here to come to his assistance, and I am not leaving until I see him." The slightly irritated secretary rang a number on the phone and spoke a few words.

"Alright, he will see you, but he isn't here. He left by the back way to avoid being seen and he took a taxi to his mansion. Here is his address." She slipped him a card and went back to her typing.

Sir Wendel was appalled at the attitude of Dr. Westcott's secretary. Something did not seem right about the way she emphasized the word 'mansion'. She was not kind, nor welcoming. That was not the Oxford way. He drove to the home of the unfortunate man and knocked on the door. A face peered out from behind a curtain then disappeared quickly.

He stood for a few more minutes, then shouted, "It is I, Sir Wendel." This time the door opened. A disheveled man answered, looked both ways, and then allowed Sir Wendel entrance.

"Sorry, my boy is keeping watch for me. I have had nothing but reporters at my door all day today. I have been summoned to court in three weeks' time and all my debts have been called in. Do you know what that means?" The man led the professor to a side room, which had been made into an office. After the door was secured, the distraught man slumped into a chair and put his hands over his face.

"I just do not know where these false accusations are coming from! I inherited this home from my father, and it has been in the family for years. I do have debts but have been faithful to pay on them every month. All my 'luxurious living' has been from the profits of selling my textbooks and not on stolen college funds! I think you know that I write curriculum for history and mathematics for college and high schools?" He looked at Sir Wendel with wild eyes, "I do not know why this is happening. It does not make any sense!"

"Calm yourself, sir, let me pray for you." not waiting for permission, he began.

"Lord, give us wisdom and peace and help us to find the answer to this dilemma. Bring back honor to this man's good name, in your name, Jesus, amen. Now let's start at the beginning. I am going to ask you questions, and I am going to take notes. With God's help this will all go away within a week. You cannot give in to fear as it will take over and render you completely useless."

"You were always a good friend, Wendel, and a wise one. I will do my best."

"Do you have any enemies?"

"Not that I know of."

"Have you kicked anyone out of Oxford lately?"

"That is one of my jobs, but they all deserved it."

"Can I get a list of everyone who has been expelled in the last year?"

"Of course." He opened his computer, found what he was looking for and pushed 'print'.

"Tell me about those who are working closely with you, the ones who know the most about your daily life."

"I have a personal secretary, Jacob Sails, he is a good lad and has a great scholarship. He knows my schedule and has access to my business bank account. He makes deposits and makes my business purchases. He has been with me for two years. Then there is my office secretary, Joan Simmons. I hired her last summer. She is a great gal, is always on top of things, and keeps the office cheerful and organized-best decision I ever made."

"How did she take the news?"

"Haven't talked to her much, just told her to hold all calls and to say that I'm not available."

"How is your wife taking this?"

"She took the youngest with her to her mom's place in Suffolk. Daniel is staying with me as he needs to finish this last year of high school. I am pretty sure he will hear about this tomorrow though, you know how bullies are!" the man groaned.

"I have some leads, my friend, but I need your direct line in case I have more questions. I will do everything I can to get to the bottom of this! Do you have anyone speaking up for you?"

"No, which isn't surprising. When the media publishes information against someone, the public believes it, and no one wants to be associated with the accused." Dr. Westcott complained.

Sir Wendel took the list that was handed to him, and the two men parted. On the way home, Sir Wendel made his plan for the next day.

He was up and out early and without breakfast. His wife knew he was on a mission.

"I just knew that television was a mistake," she muttered. The first office to get Sir Wendel's attention was the London News Station. He had briefly met the boss at a fundraiser for orphans in Africa, so at least he had an inside contact. It was always tense in a news department and crowded. The highly energetic people running around or typing madly on keyboards with the boss yelling behind a glass-door office at poor delivery boys. Not his cup of tea. Wendel made his way to the busy room, walked through the labyrinth of desks, and knocked on the office door of the news empire's boss.

"Sir Wendel, is that you? Haven't seen you since that awful fundraising dinner. How can I help you?"

"I am here on behalf of a friend whose name, I believe, has been besmirched, Vice-Chancellor Morgan Westcott. I think something is not on the up and up here, Jake."

"We double check our sources, I assure you! We have a good name to uphold too, you know," the offended man answered back.

"Could I at least talk to the reporter who delivered the story? I won't ask for sources; I just have one or two questions."

"I guess that wouldn't hurt. You will have to make it snappy though. We are starting production for tomorrow's paper."

"Are you printing more about the Vice-Chancellor?"

"Yes, everything we can get our hands on. It doesn't look good for him; I can tell you that much."

He pushed the button on his PA system, "Send in Miss Holmsted, please. You can talk in there." He pointed to a small room connected to his office.

"Probably a place where the boss can yell louder and not be heard," was the professor's thoughts.

"Yes, boss?" a short-haired, bleach blonde woman in her 30's bounded in with a stack of papers in her hands. She was slightly out of breath and obviously on a mission.

"I'm on my way out, sir, what is it?" Jack informed her that Sir Wendel wanted to ask her a few questions, then sent her into the privacy room.

"I know you are busy; I just want to ask a few questions on the story about Vice-Chancellor Morgan Westcott."

Miss Holmsted rolled her eyes. "Can't you just read the paper tomorrow?" she blurted out in a snide manner.

"I am going to help represent Dr. Westcott in court. I would like to know how reliable your source is?" was his answer.

He saw a slight, quick twinge on the side of her mouth and a flash of a frown on her forehead.

"My source is very reliable!" her offended voice declared.

"You realize that to try my client in court, your source will have to step forward?"

"I am pretty sure that is not the case. Now if you'll excuse me." She tried to push past him, but he stopped her and asked, "One last question, what is your name?"

"Virginia Holmsted," she answered while fleeing the room. He followed and took the moment to tell Jake that he was making a big mistake.

Sir Wendel, on the way home, had the time to get all his facts straight. He was pretty sure that there was only one source, that it had to be someone very close to Dr. Westcott, and pretty sure it wasn't family, which led his suspicions to the two secretaries. There was a serious discrepancy between how his friend described Miss Joan Simmons and what he had seen. That is where he would focus first. Also, it seemed that the reporter was not interested in this going to court or seeing Dr. Westcott behind bars, just that his name would become mud!

When he arrived home, after having his lunch, Sir Wendel perused the list that he had received from Dr. Westcott. He looked at each name on the list of those who had been expelled, when and why. The print-off went back two years. He looked at first and last names in case someone had masked their identity by changing either the first or the last name. A name did pop out at him. A Miss Joan Holmsted expelled for smoking an illegal substance in the gym locker room at 3:00 pm, on October 24th. He drew out his computer, googled Miss Joan Holmsted and saw all that he needed to know. He pulled up a page on Virginia Holmsted, which doubly confirmed his suspicions. Knowing that he had but a short time to halt the printing of the next day's paper, he raced out, this time forgetting his coat.

He again made it up to the newspaper's office, insisting that he had to see the big man himself. Jake was still in his office but was gathering up his belongings to carry home.

"You again?" he asked in a faltering attempt to sound cheery.

"Your reporter, Virginia Holmsted, is Joan Holmsted's sister who changed her name to Simmons and became Sir Westcott's secretary and the reporter's source! Joan was expelled from Oxford for taking an illegal substance and it is clear they do not want to take the man to court, but only ruin forever his good name!"

Jake was listening, finally. He pushed the intercom button, yelled for production to be halted, called in a reporter, and told him to type out an extensive retraction on the Vice-Chancellor's story. He set down the pile that was in his arms and sat down hard on the well-cushioned chair.

"Do you know what this means?" he demanded. "We could be seriously sued!"

"If I may make a suggestion, I will talk to Dr. Westcott and try to talk him out of a lawsuit, but in the meantime, I really think that having the entire story come out would be helpful. Also, you need to get the whole truth from Dr. Westcott about his earnings, his inherited possessions, and the income he receives from his writing of textbooks."

Jake's head was in his hands, moving back and forth, "I need a holiday!"

Sir Wendel called his friend's private number, relayed the information he had dug up, and then handed the phone to Jake. For fifteen minutes Jake took notes, nodded his head, and thanked the head of Oxford University for his patience and for his forgiveness. It wasn't a pleasant task, being humble like that, but he did it well.

Jake lifted his head in time to see the reporter, Virginia Holmsted, sit down at her computer.

"Miss Holmsted, in my office, now!" the announcement went loudly and sharply over the intercom.

Sir Wendel took his cue and made a hasty exit. At home, he immediately packed up the newly purchased television, put it in his car and took it back to the store. He did not want to be an ostrich and stick his head in the sand. He just wanted commercial-free news, which he could find elsewhere. He was thankful though, that this bit of technology had saved the day for Dr. Westcott.

CHAPTER 13

War Then Peace

"Dad, do you have a minute? I need to talk!" Winston sounded a bit desperate, so his father made a lunch date. They sat on a campus bench, eating the sandwiches his mother had made while Winston shared his frustrations.

"This is my junior year at Oxford, and they stick a thug of a freshmen in my room with me. We aren't allowed to put in for a transfer for the first two weeks of the semester. I am stuck with the hulk! He is a 6-foot 3 inch, red-headed Irish bloke who won't clean and who has a chip on his shoulder. I may have to come home for a while!"

"Did you ask him to clean?"

"Yes, and he shoved everything under his bed. There was no shame on his face either!" Winston tossed his sandwich back into the bag; he had lost his appetite.

"And do you know what else? I was talking to this girl, and he kept giving me the stink eye. The next time he practically threatened me!"

"Was it his girlfriend?"

"Don't think so, I think he wants her to be. She has an Irish accent too. Then I walk into the room, and I said that it smelled. He nearly blew a cork! He had just sprayed on some Irish cologne, but I didn't say it stunk! When he first moved in, he asked for a bite of my pizza and then took a whole piece! Dad, I have never been so irritated with someone in my whole life!"

"Now Son, maybe the problem is in defining your terms. Maybe clean to him is getting everything out of sight. Maybe that is how he was raised. Maybe his mom shouted that company was coming over and they rushed around shoving things in every nook and cranny. Also, perhaps this girl he likes has been in his sights since he was in kindergarten. Maybe that is why he came to Oxford. He sees your handsome face hanging around and he sees his dreams evaporate. Tell me, did you talk to her just because you saw that it annoyed him?"

"Maybe." Wendel smirked.

"That passive aggressive thing that people do is quite naughty you know. Those non-communicative, sly, and vindictive jabs do not build relationships. And have you considered that maybe, in his culture, a bite may mean a piece? I think you should start over and make sure you tell him that you are not interested in his girlfriend."

"I'm sure you are right. I shouldn't allow those hateful feelings to take over." Winston winced and finished his lunch.

That night Winston arrived at his dorm room carrying an extra-large pepperoni pizza.

"Hey, I bought us a pizza, are you hungry?" Seamus Milligan hesitated but grunted and grabbed two pieces.

"I just want you to know that when I came into the room the other night and wondered what smelled. I really meant to say, what smells good. It is Irish Spring? I really need to get some of that. No wonder you are a hit with the girls!"

Seamus looked up and with his mouth full sputtered, "Old Spice."

"Ah, good stuff. I'll have to get me some." Winston was purposely flattering his roommate. "And by the way, you have a pretty girlfriend, what's her name? I have my eyes on a girl named Mary."

"Um, she's not my girlfriend, and her name is Bonnie."

"So, what degree are you working toward?" Winston asked, trying his hardest to connect.

"I got a sports scholarship, rugby, but I'm going for my music degree."

"No kidding! Tell me about your musical talents!" Winston wasn't faking his surprise.

"Well, I play the flute and sing and write music." Seamus answered after gulping down his last bite of pizza.

"I have always wanted to play the flute; do you think you could teach me?" Winston impetuously asked.

Seamus, pulling out his flute from under the bed, said that he would try to if he had time.

"Do you want to hear a song I wrote?"

"Sure!" Winston sat down and the large fingered boy prepared his instrument and began to play. It was a different sound than what Winston had ever heard before. It was mysterious and slow yet sounded like wind flowing over the moors. At least that is how Winston described it to his father the next day.

Then out of the blue Seamus set the flute down and with the most beautiful tenor voice Winston had ever heard, he began to sing a sorrowful and melodic love song.

"There was a girl o'er in Killarney, all silver and white and free
As a dove she went a flitting, and I followed as close as could be
She dangled that love line before me, the foolish young man that
I was
Til at last I cut loose and stop tagging
Like a dog on a leash that one does
Oh, but I still love that little wee Lassie, my heart will ne'er
forget
But ne'er will I let a wee Lassie
Dangle me on with a lie, no ne'er again 'til the day, 'til the day
that I die!"

Winston sat mesmerized with his mouth open. He was stunned. He was thinking, this guy was so good; he belonged on stage! It only got better.

"Hey, want to see something else?" Seamus didn't wait for an answer, pulled out a cassette player, set it up and turned it on. He cranked up the music and started dancing! The *thud, thud, thud,* was sure to make the dorm leaders think about seismic activity. Seamus kicked and twirled, he held his hands in a fist at his side and the only motion was in his lower body. He went on for 15 minutes until someone pounded on the door.

"Seamus, I have never heard or seen anything so marvelous! Skip rugby, you need to go on stage and travel the world. My goodness, you have more talent than I have ever seen in my life!" Winston truly meant every word. Seamus grew a bit uncomfortable with all the accolades.

"Would you like to be famous?" asked Winston.

"I never thought much about it, but yes, I think that would be grand!"

That night Winston fell into bed figuring out how he could manage being Seamus' agent and finish school at the same time. The next day he met with his dad and couldn't stop talking about his roommate.

"I guess that conflict was settled?"

"Dad, you are not listening. This guy has got to be discovered. He is going to be famous!"

"Son, are you sure he has what it takes to get all that attention and stay humble? Would he succumb to temptation and lose his good morals? Could he handle the constant travels? What about this girl he likes? Would he not prefer to settle down and get married and entertain his wife and children instead?" Winston felt like a wet blanket had just been thrown over his shoulders.

The next day Winston stopped in at the Oxford University office and talked to the secretary. "Are we having any productions or talent type shows this year?"

"The music department has three productions on the schedule and the theater department has two. Haven't been given the names yet."

Winston went to the professor over the productions department and asked what was planned for the year. "Carousel, the musical, will be the first one that we present, just before the winter break. Then in the spring we are doing a play from a John Wayne movie, 'The Quiet Man.'"

Winston groaned, "Professor, my roommate is the most talented man I know, and he would be perfect in these productions. He can sing, dance and he plays the flute! He is getting a music degree, but he didn't know to join the acting class!"

"Maybe we can rearrange his schedule. Bring him in tonight at 7:00 and I will see what he can do, and we will see what can be done."

Winston brought Seamus to the theater and made him do exactly what he had shown him the night before. The teacher was impressed and wanted to talk to Seamus some more. Winston sneaked out of the room.

Sir Wendel, Winston, and Ruth sat around the dinner table on Saturday night and Winston excitedly told his parents how Seamus dropped band to get into theater.

"He can take band next semester instead of speech class. If nothing else, he will make Oxford look stunning!"

The next day on Winston's desk was a bottle of Old Spice and a note of thank

CHAPTER 14

The Wrong Choice

The Nutcracker Suite ballet was something Sir Wendell took his wife, Ruth, to every Christmas. It had become a tradition. One, which Sir Wendel wished he could replace. They dressed in their Christmas finest and went to the opera house. An usher led them to the front row. Sometimes being well known does not pay off. But when the music began, Sir Wendel would forget all his complaints. He loved the Russian Peter Tchaikovsky's lively and dramatic works, and yet dozed off through the more sedate movements. He decided that he would keep the tradition after all. Sitting in the front row also made it difficult to escape quickly when the production ended. He and his wife talked to several people around them that they knew or at least saw every year, same time, and same place.

It was nearly their turn to follow the crowd down the aisle when a young lady came up to him.

"Hello, Professor. You probably don't remember me. I was in the class when you were the substitute for Philosophy three years ago. I really liked what you said. I based my thesis on one of your ideas. But that is not why I wanted to talk to you." The young lady noticed she was going to miss her opportunity if she didn't hurry.

"My name is Sophie, I was the clarinetist in the orchestra tonight, and anyway I have a problem. I need some help. Could I meet with you sometime at the university?"

"Lunchtime tomorrow, what about noon at the library?" Sir Wendel did not like to procrastinate. The happy student thanked him profusely.

He arrived at the library early to peruse the section containing books about Siberia to see if he had overlooked any. His eyes glanced over to a particular table and halted. The same young lady, Sophie, was seated and was attempting to read, but there were three distracting male stalkers surrounding her. He watched for a few minutes and realized that she was not happy about the attention. He walked over, introduced himself as a guardian to 'Miss Sophie' and asked the young men what their intentions were. They stuttered and stammered and began to gather up their things.

"Sirs," piped the professor, "I regret to tell you that this young woman is completely off limits and if you dare to impose upon her time again, I will contact the Dean of Students."

"Yes, sir," resounded the guilty lads and they dashed off.

"How did you know, Professor, that they were my problem?" questioned Sophie.

"I am very glad that I deduced correctly, or you would not be pleased with me right now," laughed Sir Wendel. They conversed for a few minutes, and he walked out and headed to the parking lot.

"Dad!" shouted Winston, who ran over and grabbed his dad's arm. "Could you come to Latin class with me? There is someone I would like you to meet!"

"Oh, dear," thought Wendel, but agreed to go. The class met in the theater.

"Dad, we are practicing for the Latin play that we will perform in a month. I really want you and Mom to attend!"

Wendel didn't have the heart to tell him that he would be in Russia at that time.

A young woman came up behind Winston and he pulled her in front of his dad.

"Dad this is Mary Morris. Her dad is in shipping, and she is getting a psychology degree. Mary this is my dad, Sir Wendel Salomon." The nice-to-meet-you went both ways, and the class began.

"Sir Wendel! Would you like to greet the class?" the over enthusiastic Latin teacher asked.

"Salvete, discipulae et discipuli et Magistra." Sir Wendel greeted.

"Salve, Magister," was the reply. The students gathered on the stage and Sir Wendel snuck out as soon as he could without being noticed. His heart was troubled about the girl he was introduced to. It wasn't that he was so close-minded as to be affected by tattoos, rings in the nose, metal balls on the lip and tongue, short skirts, and low necks. When it comes to one's children, you need to trust God, but what was bothering him? He realized it was how she avoided looking him in the eye.

He made a beeline for home, for office, for computer and typed in 'Mary Morris', then 'shipping company owner Morris'. He found a phone number and called the man.

"Hello, this is Professor Wendel Salomon from Oxford University. No, nothing's wrong, I just have a few questions. I am calling on behalf of my son who has taken a liking to your daughter. I am just wondering what you think about this?" Wendel held the phone away from his ear as the man was laughing so loud it hurt.

"Sir, tell your son to forget his infatuation. My daughter is already taken. She is engaged to a young man in Portugal and the wedding occurs right after graduation. Tell your son that I'm sorry!"

"Thank you. And yes, I will tell him." Wendel left a message at Winston's dorm inviting him to lunch the following Saturday.

"Mom is making your favorite," he had said. The father thought a favorite food would soften the blow. Winston called back and asked if he could bring Mary.

"Son, can we ask her to come on Sunday?" replied Sir Wendel.

Ruth cooked roast beef and Yorkshire pudding, and the table was set when Winston arrived.

"What is the occasion, Mom? Dad?" Winston was suspicious and the room seemed tense.

"I don't want to ruin a good dinner with bad news or with you being angry with me, but I did just a bit of snooping and found out that Mary is engaged to a Portuguese fellow. The wedding is right after graduation." Wendel let out the sordid news in one long breath, then both he and Ruth held their breath.

"I'm fine, Dad, let's eat." The couple visibly relieved, exhaled.

After dinner, father and son retired to the office.

"Son, I am preparing to take a trip to Siberia. I am ready to plan out the trains that I will be taking. Mom will go, of course, and I will leave her in Estonia to visit her family."

"Dad, you really should wait until July for three reasons. One, I also really want to go with you and connect with my roots. Two, you do not want to go when the tundra is still frozen, your joints won't work. Three, I can be a big help in research and actually use my degree. This means you would have to wait a few months longer, but I believe it would be worth the wait!"

Winston continued, "My roots are your roots. I also want to know where the name Salomon is from, and this may be the last father-son bonding time we may ever have. Also, you know how much you detest the cold and snowy weather. It would be difficult to get really warmed up in Siberia. Plus, you would have to go buy all kinds of expensive winter clothing. Finally, I am going to have to find a real job so this may be the last trip I take to see the grandparents. Who knows how long they are going to live, and I am sure they would love to see me. So, this really matters to them and to me. Let's hear it, Dad, what do you say?"

Surprised, Sir Winston finally asked, "How did you know that I was going to Siberia to search for my roots?"

"Come on, Dad, I have been coming in here since I was a kid and looking through those diaries. I also read your notes. You never did lock your desk, so I didn't think it was off limits."

"Ah, well, you have a very good argument and I guess it wouldn't hurt to wait a bit longer. You can also help me plan the trip and schedule the itinerary."

The night of the Latin play found Sir Wendel and Ruth seated in the Oxford theater and fanning themselves with the program. It was an unusually warm evening and the room seemed rather stuffy.

"It looks like Winston plays the part of a centurion and his ex-girlfriend is to be a martyred Christian. I guess Christians are accepted in schools as long as they are martyred!" Sir Wendel sarcastically stated.

The play began. Some students were in togas, some wore suits of armor and carried swords and one was in a Cesar's outfit with a laurel of leaves encircling his head. The actors marched back and forth on stage repeating memorized lines. Then filed in a group of 'Christian' prisoners wearing the simple shepherd garb reminiscent of a nativity scene. The interpretation was in the program.

Wendel laid his head back and envisioned the plight of the first century Christians. He saw their bravery in the face of death, their serene countenance as they were fed to the lions or hung on crosses. He found himself strangely emotional and wondering if he would have been so brave. He thought about how the modern world thinks that they are so far from those barbaric ways of the past; yet at this very moment a greater persecution was occurring around the world. He breathed a short prayer, "What can I do to help?"

"Sequāmur Christum etiam ad mortem!" shouted Mary Morris. Wendel jumped.

She continued, "Prō Christō patiāmur!"

Wendel whispered the interpretation, "Let us follow Christ even unto death. Let us suffer for Christ."

She had meant those lines, he could tell. This was more than acting; this was a passion for the Christ that Miss Morris knew. He smiled and realized once again that man looks at the outward, but God looks at the heart.

"Itaque omnēs hōs Chrīstiānōs gladiō animadvertī placet," shouted Winston.

"And so, it is decreed that all these Christians be punished by the sword," thoughtfully translated Sir Wendel.

"Well done, my son," congratulated Sir Wendel to Winston after the production. "That was probably the best acting I have ever seen."

He ended with these words, "Ā cūnctīs nōs, quaesumus, Domine, mentis et corporis dēfende perīculīs."

CHAPTER 15

A Good Name: Better Than Riches

"Hey, Dad, just calling to say that you will never guess who I ran into today! I had to buy a notebook so went to town and I recognized someone from high school. It was Guy Westin! You know, the senior who had his teeth bashed in by Bobby Ashe. Remember? Bobby was terrible at playing baseball, we all were. Coach was teaching us, and the first time Bobby hits the ball it flies hard into Guy's mouth. Ha-ha, it was really terrible, sorry for laughing. The most humorous part is Guy had been teasing Bobby mercilessly, mostly about his weight. No matter what Bobby did, he made a joke about it. Guy was a sponsored student and I think he did it to make himself feel better, but he also had the worst buck teeth I have ever seen. He couldn't even shut his lips. He was out of school for two weeks and when he returned, he had the best-looking teeth, all paid for by the school's insurance. If I recall clearly, Bobby apologized to Guy and Guy apologized back.

"Anyway, Guy is a tour bus driver and has a 7-year-old boy who is so cute, has normal teeth, and is very plump!"

"Ah, yes, I remember that day very well. So glad he is doing well. Thanks for calling, Son."

Sir Wendel climbed the stairs to his bedroom, to have his lie-down. He rarely napped, but he found that in a prone position, he could ponder, plan, and pray with better concentration. His son's call was bringing back the memory of that day when he received a call from Principal Flax:

"No, Winston is doing fine, I am calling because I have a problem that just occurred with one of my students, Seymour Fox. It isn't a police matter, just mostly a conundrum."

"I will be there right away," promised Sir Wendel. He had remembered Winston telling him about the problems Seymour was causing. He did things like, hang gym shorts on the statue in front of the school and stick gum on the water fountains. He was loud and obnoxious. The boys made puns from their names 'Flax flogs Fox' and "Fox flees from Flax' and 'Flax fails Fox.' The school, Cambridge Classical High School, was an all-boys school and very expensive. One month's tuition covered about half a teacher's salary for the month. This resulted in the principal being very forgiving toward naughty students.

"Thank you for coming, Sir Wendel. Walk with me."

They headed past the locker hallway to the hallway that led to the classrooms. At the end of the hallway was a mass of broken glass covering the floor.

"As you can see, we had an issue this morning, but I can't seem to find out what happened. We didn't clean it up so you could see it. We have half an hour before classes let out."

111

They walked to the end of the hall and Sir Wendel carefully studied every detail. It was a large corner trophy case, a really fancy one that sat about three feet above ground on wooden lion-claw legs. It had set prominently in the corner with trophies and ribbons displayed on glass shelves.

Principal Flax described the incident.

"I saw Seymour come in late for school and followed him to this hall for the purpose of rebuking him. Before I could get to him, he put his skateboard on the ground and headed quickly down the hall. I am not one to raise my voice, so I just watched him. When he got to the corner, at that exact same moment, the glass shattered. And he just kept going around the corner then slid and fell. He says that the shock of it caused him to lose his balance. He is a troublemaker, but this is the one time he insisted that he had nothing to do with it."

"Was there anything in his hands?"

"No, he was so late for class that he decided to skip going to his locker and just borrow paper and pencil from a classmate."

"Do you believe him?"

"Yes, I somehow do. But it does seem too coincidental to not be on purpose."

"Is it important to find out what happened?"

"One of the parents made and donated the case, and for that reason I feel I must figure out what has happened."

"Were there any other students in the hallway at that time?"

"Now that you mention it, there were two at their lockers at the end of the first hallway and one standing close to me with a ruler that he dropped. Yes, I remember who that was."

After ten more minutes, Sir Wendel said that the mess could be removed. He then met with the lad in question in the principal's office. He didn't find anything beneficial from the meeting except that he too found the boy's claim of innocence hard to deny.

After the rubble had been removed, Sir Wendel scrutinized, with a magnifying glass, the entire spot where the case had been. He noticed a small hole in the wall where the glass had touched. He then counted the paces it took to get from one end of the hall to the other.

"Mr. Flax, may I ask you a few questions?" Sir Wendel queried. They walked into the quiet hallway.

"I see that this middle wall that divides the two hallways looks newer than the rest of the building and it doesn't reach the ceiling."

"Oh, yes, this school was a donation from the city. It had been a hospital about a hundred years ago. We had nowhere to put the lockers, so this wall was built, and the lockers inserted."

"Do you have the right to open lockers?" asked Sir Wendel.

"Of course," replied the principal.

Wendel counted the one hundred fifty paces it had taken to go down the other hallway and stopped in front of locker 304.

"Can you open this one?" It was a neat and clean locker. Wendel searched it thoroughly.

"That is Matthew Daniel's locker, good kid, never causes a problem," insisted the principal. Sir Wendel motioned to the one next to it. He searched five lockers, but on the sixth one hit pay dirt.

"Dirk Danger's," the stunned principal managed to mutter. The locker was covered with drawings and magazine cutouts that were anything but loving. Sir Wendel began to methodically go through every piece of paper, thumb through every book and read every note written on every Pee-Chee.

"Look here, Mr. Flax." Sir Wendel held up a Pee-Chee with the words, 'I will get even with you, Fox!'

"It looks like we found a motive."

Mr. Flax was completely in the dark. He didn't even want to ask how those words related to a broken trophy case.

Wendel finished pulling everything out of the small space, he then pulled out the shelves and managed to pull out the back panel of the locker. There, right at eye level, was a small hole.

"The method is clear. One boy stood near you and as soon as Fox passed the case, he signaled by throwing the ruler. Then the other two boys jammed the drill into the glass. The open locker door would have hidden from your view the books, the shelves, and the back of the locker that had been pulled out. When you went down to see what had happened, the boys quickly replaced everything.

"We found the means, now we have to find the evidence, which would be in the shape of a small drill. I suggest we confront Mr. Danger in the classroom before he can ditch the device."

Dirk was found to have in his possession a very small, handheld dentist's drill, which he had used to drill through the plasterboard and hammer into the glass at the exact moment Seymour had skated by. The rest was history. Dirk was expelled along with his three accomplices, and their parents had to reimburse the school for replacement of the trophy case. Sir Wendel was wrapping it up, shaking hands with Principal Flax, when in walked a panicked gym teacher holding a towel over a boy's face and yelling to call an ambulance. The coach proceeded to explain how a baseball had unfortunately smashed into the lad's mouth.

Sir Wendel had grabbed the towel as he could tell the coach was beginning to swoon. Some people can't handle the sight of blood. A short, pudgy boy stood about fifteen feet away, looking very forlorn. After the ambulance left, Sir Wendel asked the lad to show him the restroom where he could wash his hands. The boy broke down sobbing saying how sorry he was.

"Did you do it on purpose?"

"No, I didn't even know I could hit a ball!" he replied.

"Is he a good friend?" Wendel asked.

"No, he hates me because I'm fat," the boy answered.

"What is your name, son?"

"Bobby Ashe."

"Listen Bobby, this was purely and simply an accident. When that boy comes back to school, just go up to him and tell him that you are sorry. I promise that when that happens you will feel better. Accidents happen," encouraged Sir Wendel.

Wendel, eight years later, wondered what had happened to little Bobby, Dirk Danger, and Seymour Fox. He chuckled and wondered if having girls in the mix would have made the boys behave just a little better.

"A good study," he mumbled out loud.

CHAPTER 16

Playing Chess

"Life is a lot like playing chess, my boy," explained Sir Wendel to his son Winston. "This is most evident when butting heads with someone who holds an opposite viewpoint, especially when the outcome of that viewpoint has a result of life or death." Winston knew his father was about to delve into one of his battlefield stories.

"You were just a lad at the time, and I was teaching full-time at the university when I received a call from the science department. The biology teacher, Professor Byron Mock, had come down with the flu and I was needed to take his class for the next two weeks. Well, the schedule fit with mine and I was happy to oblige. The next day I picked up the syllabus and began to look over the assignments. Winston, I was thrilled to find out what I was about to be presenting to a class of biology students. Can you guess?"

"Evolution?"

"Right you are, and I was going to thoroughly enjoy myself. Being a knighted war hero gives me a kind of tenure with Oxford. I can be myself and present truth as I see fit. But I saw it as a chess game. I had to be cunning and crafty. I had to allow the students to come to their own conclusions. So, with the intention of being a covert influence, I began to prepare."

"How did it go?"

"Better than expected. I know of three of those students who became leaders in the church, and I periodically hear from a few or run into one or two here and there. I can say with humility that not one of that group was unaffected by those two weeks of washing away the fallacies of the scientific community. It was a cold autumn day..." Sir Wendel began his narration.

"...I am Professor Wendel Salomon, and I am here while Professor Mock is out with the flu. The topics we are to discuss in the next two weeks are some of my favorites. I think there are certain things about evolution, or Darwinism, I will be able to share with you that perhaps you have never thought of before. I am sure you know that creationists have a different view of how the world began, but do you know on several points we agree? Yes, it is true.

"We both believe that there was a beginning, and it began with water, unless you follow the Big Bang theory, in which case it began with power. Both believe that what is seen began with the unseen. They agree not everything came into being at the exact same moment, creationists have birds and fish on one day and animals and man on the next, evolutionists say there were billions and billions of years between creatures. And both believe animals and man are made from the same stuff.

Both believe in an organized universe, and both agree with the great scientists like Kepler, Galileo, and Newton and their well-known laws. The difference, however, concerns one single point. Darwinists believe in a random, unplanned, unorganized beginning and creationists believe that a grand designer with a grand design planned and created the universe."

With this, Sir Wendel paused his narration, "Winston, can you see how I began the 'game' with the pawns. Pawns are unassuming, non-threatening pieces which are considered to be neither offensive nor defensive. They make short moves, one step at a time. I moved both side's pawns and no one was on guard or preparing for a battle. Those students did not really know where I stood on the matter."

He continued, "So with an almighty designer, there would be no problem taking six days to complete creation. If there had been a creator, for the argument, then there would be very specific things you would notice about the world and the universe. You would not see different evolved species in specific layers of geological digs, especially major animal groups from a Cambrian explosion. Animal breeders would never be able to come up with new species of animals, nor could scientists create life in a petri dish. We still may not find dinosaurs buried with humans. But we would find design in everything from the smallest creature all the way up to the way the universe moves."

"Winston, this is where I moved the knight, two steps forward and one sidewise. They still are not quite sure where I stand, because most of them do not know their own belief system. So, I continue.

"...It was quite unfortunate though, that the subtitle to Darwin's book was, The Preservation of Favored Races in the Struggle for Life, in which lies the horrific roots of racism. This is the belief that we as humans are separated by race. This philosophy is not based in science of course. It spurned Stalin's,

Mao's, and Hitler's actions against so-called inferior races. Now you, as brilliant, truth-seeking Oxford students, agree with science that there is only a .012 percent difference between the genetics of cultural groups and these have to do with eye color, skin color, and other external characteristics. Maybe you do not know this, that there are actually more differences genetically within the same group than between two groups. Maybe that is why sometimes genetic oddities occur when royalty or isolated people groups do not marry outside of their gene pool…

"Can you see, Winston, how I took my bishop halfway across the board? Let's see, where was I?

"…Just because so much of the Bible's history has been dug up by archaeologists, does that prove that the entire Bible is true? Abraham's Ur, Jonah's Nineveh, Joshua's Jericho, and King Solomon's cities of Hazor, Megiddo, and Gezer have all been excavated. In addition, many ancient writings of ancient cultures tell of a worldwide flood including the Gilgamesh Epic, of which I am sure you have read…

"See, Winston, how I brought my castle straight up as far as I could bring it."

"Yes, Dad, but are they moving?"

"No, but I am making moves for them, and I can tell you, so far I am winning."

He continued, "…So the history of the Bible isn't in question here, it is only those first two chapters in Genesis that we debate with the creationist group. At this time, I feel that I must bring to the discussion a colleague of mine, a Dr. Willard Libby, who has come up with a type of dating called carbon dating. I have thoroughly gone over his studies, and he assumes the carbon-14 to carbon-12 ratio in the atmosphere has always been the same. If this were true, then this type of dating would be accurate for up to 80,000 years. But for this atmospheric equilibrium to be constant, the amount of carbon-14 created would have to equal the amount of its removal. With his assumption that the earth is millions of years old, and that the earth began with no carbon-14, it would take 30,000 years to build up to the state of equilibrium. I saw his notes and he has failed to report that there indeed is a discrepancy with his figures."

"There is not a constant ratio of carbon-14 to carbon-12. There is a difference of 2.7 atoms per gram per minute. Equilibrium has yet to occur and may never occur. He almost listened to me, but someday some scientist may take his work, repeat the experiments, and then publish the correct findings. I also puzzle at the possibility that the magnetic field, most likely stronger in the past, had done a better job at deflecting cosmic rays which play a huge part in how much C-14 is found in organisms. The stronger the field, the less C-14 would be found."

"Furthermore, the earth's magnetic field has been carefully measured for over 140 years and it has been noted that the rate of decay has a half-life of 1,400 years. So, 1,400 years ago the magnetic field was twice as strong, four times as strong 2,800 years ago and so on. The conclusion of this is that 10,000 years ago the magnetic field would have been as great as a magnetic star. Scientifically, the earth could not be older than 6,000. This was determined in the 1970's by Professor Dr. Thomas Barnes who noted that the main part of the earth's magnetic field decays at a rate of 5% per century. His theory was that a 'freely decaying electric current' in the earth's metallic core caused the earth's magnetic field."

"His calculations showed that this current couldn't have been decaying for more than 10,000 years or its starting strength would have been large enough to melt the earth. Archaeological measurements reveal that the field was 40% stronger in AD

1000 than today. It is now time for scientists to figure this one out. But let us not be discouraged, my friends, and move on."

"I moved my queen on that move, Winston, but let me show you where my next move took me." Sir Wendel added.

"…We do have conflicts with the theory that the earth is millions of years old. One being the proven fact that the moon moves away from the earth at the rate of about inch every year. We are seeing that if we go back 1.2 billion years, the moon would be right next to the earth. At one-third the distance to the earth, the gravitational pull would drown the earth with tidal water twice a day. The moon's dust is another way to determine the age of the universe.

"Meteorites and material from their disintegration has been falling to earth at a constant rate. At 5 billion years old the earth would have 182 feet of dust covering it. The Apollo astronauts should have found the same thickness on the moon. Their expectation of sinking into very thick and dangerous dust was quelled three years before when in 1966 NASA landed five Surveyor spacecraft on the moon to discover only a few inches of dust. The scientific community fell silent as to why their expectations weren't true. Unfortunately for them, the thickness of the dust compared to how much settles in a year, revealed the earth's age at less than 10,000 years.

"If fossil fuel deposits are actually hundreds of millions of years old, the oil and natural gas that are held at high pressures in the underground reservoirs would have leaked out to the surface long ago. The 2nd law of Thermodynamics states that left to itself every system will move from complex to the simple, from order to disorder, from organization to disorganization. This law is universal and certain. Isaac Asimov noted, that as far as we know, all changes are in the direction of increasing entropy, disorder, randomness, and of running down. Evolution requires the opposite of this, an upward change.

121

Death and aging are evidence of this, even in living systems. Yes, we have seeds becoming trees and embryos becoming developed humans, but that is because of an inherited DNA in each living structure. Even a building needs a blueprint.

"Abiogenesis, the idea that living comes from non-living, should still be able to be seen today or at least reproduced in a laboratory. Even if we could form a protein molecule, it would never reproduce itself. Mutations, another evolutionary required mechanism, are random, rare, mostly lethal, or at least nearly always harmful. Rarely do we find a positive result from a mutation.

"The Big Bang theory is the idea that the universe was compacted and held at different temperatures, then exploded. The scientists following this theory have run into a problem because every part of the universe has the same temperature as measured by electromagnetic radiation. The differences are only one part per 10 to the fifth. There hasn't been enough time for light to exchange between two points in the universe to create this uniform temperature. The scientists are trying to figure this out.

"We do see that Einstein is correct when looking at disintegrating comets, decaying magnetic fields, hot blue stars, and rotating spiral galaxies, which he claimed cannot last billions of years longer. His conclusion was that this expanding universe had a beginning, and it will have an ending, also similar to a creationist's view. I'm sure none of us think that the earth will endure that long anyway.

"Next time we meet we will talk about zircons and how they contain large amounts of helium, how coal and diamonds can contain carbon-14, how salt is entering the sea quicker than it is leaving it, how comets lose mass when they pass the sun, how no erosion is found between geological layers, and more about the increasing human mutation problem and how it affects lifespan. Thank you, class, you are dismissed…"

"Winston, I see by your face that you think I went too far, that I confused the group, and that they were not yet at an intellectual level to receive these details. I, on the other hand, think they probably became aware that they are not completely aware."

"You are probably right, Dad. I bet they slunk out of that class and wished Dr. Mock was back!"

"Except that I had a few come up afterwards and asked for my bibliography references so they could study on their own. That was my goal all along. Although, I did have a smart one in the group who asked…"

"Hey, Prof, what about radiometric dating?"

"Good question! (I answered). This is also called radioisotope dating and refers to the dating of igneous rock, or what comes up and cools from a volcano. This is measuring what is called the half-life, which is the changing from one isotope of an element to another. Without going into too much detail, as we are nearly out of time, the problem with this type of dating is that when testing on rocks that we were certain the age of, the result was a date ranging from 0.5 million to 2.8 million years. The results were not uniform. Now this is a terrible embarrassment to the scientific community who, of course, are tied closely to the evolutionary model. Another type of dating, the isochronal method, has the same type of issue, when testing hot-out-of-the-volcano rocks, they are shown to be very old. We must make sure our experimental methods prove true on rocks we do know the age of, like those from newly erupted volcanoes. The problem is that science makes assumptions about the initial conditions of the samples, about the amount of primary and secondary elements in a sample, about whether that sample has been altered by nature, and about whether the half-life or decay

123

rate of the primary isotope has remained constant since the rock's formation. We cannot be certain that the earth's history has not been changed by eruptions, floods, or changes in temperature and pressure which would indeed have toyed with the results of any type of dating process. I am sure we all agree that we cannot date fossils using rocks then proceed to date rocks by using fossils-this is called circular reasoning. It is also interesting that textbooks dated the evolutionary columns 100 years before the radiometric dating method. My question is how did they match those dates? A lab that tests those rocks will only date them if the scientist gives his guess on the age. This is how they dated moon rocks. Rocks from Nigeria were tested with four different methods of dating and the results were embarrassing—between 2 million and 750 million years!

"And worse, when they don't like a particular date, it is discarded. That is not an acceptable method for us scientific thinking Oxford people. I think that maybe a few of you would like to rise to the challenge and become the earth scientists of the future and solve these very perplexing problems...

"Checkmate, Winston."

"Looks like you got it all off your chest, Dad. I am sure they were hoping that you weren't giving a pop-quiz during the next class."

"No, but I answered more questions and had discussion about marine fossils being found at high altitudes, extinct amphibians being found in Texas, and the mammoth graveyards in Siberia. We covered the evidence for a worldwide flood that seems to give evidence as to why fossil formations seem to show a sudden entrapment and rapid burial. I talked about fossil graveyards of both extinct animals and bones from animals still living being found all over the world which is further evidence for a large global catastrophe. I never heard back from Professor Mock, and I rather think he avoided me after that."

CHAPTER 17

Rehabilitation

Over the years, since before his mother had passed away, Sir Wendel tried to visit The Recovery Centre, a place for people of all ages who needed to recover or convalesce after surgery. His mother had spent a few months at this facility, and Wendel enjoyed talking to the patients. He decided one day that his visit was long overdue and with nothing on his schedule, headed out after breakfast. He was at the desk adding his name to the list of visitors when a nurse came by. She seemed to try to discourage his visit.

"I am sorry, sir, but the patients are very tired today, and maybe another day would be better?"

Sir Wendel looked at his watch, "It is 11:00 in the morning, aren't the patients getting ready for lunch?"

Sir Wendel knew the routine and he knew it hadn't changed in the twenty years since he had been coming.

"Well, sir, you see, they get restless at night so around 4:00 a.m. we give them melatonin, a natural sleep enhancer and sometimes they sleep until 1:00 in the afternoon."

"You give this to them at 4:00 a.m.?" Sir Wendel asked.

"Yes sir," she answered.

"Well, if you do not mind, I will walk around and see if anyone feels like talking."

The nurse quickly disappeared and Wendel had an odd feeling that all was not right. Was the nurse giving him information on purpose? He went from room to room until he found a young girl in a body cast whose eyes were wide open. She was watching television.

"Knock, knock." Sir Wendel said as he peeked into the room.

"Who's there?" the girl replied.

They introduced themselves, discussed how long she had been there (4 weeks), what had happened to her (car accident), how old she was (16), and what school she attended (Henrietta Barnett School).

"I am so bored!" she complained while trying to get into a comfortable position. "My family can't be here except on the weekends, and I have two more months to go. My friends live quite far away so they only come once a month. I watch TV all day long and I've started counting commercials. There are usually eight during each commercial break!"

"You go to one of the best schools in London, so I've heard." Wendel was trying to change the subject to a more positive one.

"You are right, nearly everyone gets A's on their report cards, but I have been struggling to keep up and I did not get any A's!"

"Why do you think that is, Rebecca?" Sir Wendel asked.

"My memory is not very good. My mates study all night before a test and ace it. I do the same, but I'm in such a fog that I cannot function well. My parents are starting to get on my case about it too. That is the one good thing about the car wreck; they stopped talking about grades!" Rebecca was not at all being cheered by the professor's visit.

"You know that there are different types of learning styles, maybe we should discover which one you have." Sir Wendel was ready to begin a counseling session, but the girl only frowned.

"Who are you? I was taught not to talk to strangers." She began to reach for the nurse's call button when Sir Wendel whipped out his card. Her hand relaxed.

"I would love to go to Oxford! But with my grades, it isn't likely."

Sir Wendel was in his element, and he began one of his famous speeches.

"I have helped many students reach their goals. I am pretty sure I can aid you in accomplishing a speedy progress and if you comply, I assure you that straight A's are in your future. I think that we should first work on your memory. This week I want you to think about a different school topic for 15 minutes each day, and I want you to review everything that you remember about that topic. How does that sound?"

"That's easy, what about the rest of the day?"

"I am going to come back tomorrow and bring you things to work on and I will want a review on what you remembered. I'll see you tomorrow." Sir Wendel slipped out in time to see lunch starting to be handed out. He noted what was being served, macaroni and cheese, chocolate pudding, a dinner roll and a scoop of creamed corn and a diet soda. He followed behind the nurses and watched them try to wake up the patients.

"Don't you think that giving them sleeping pills at 4:00 in the morning is counterproductive?" He asked.

The nurse nodded and said that she had to follow orders. Most of the patients were elderly, but there were several that were not. He chatted a bit with them and invited them to a get together the following day at 11:30 a.m. The nurse remarked that he had better get permission.

"Don't worry, as a supporter of this facility I am quite sure the head nurse will allow me to spend some time encouraging the patients. I will head over there now."

Wendel walked into Nurse Needle's office and took a chair. She seemed genuinely happy to see him.

"So good to see you, Sir Wendel! It has been a while, hasn't it?"

"Yes, I have failed in my duties as the main cheerer-upper around here. Good to be back though. I have already connected to the student, Rebecca, and am going to try to increase her test scores. I want to play a game tomorrow in the main room. Also, I would like to mention that a 10 mg dose of melatonin is far too much in my estimation." Sir Wendel was hoping not to offend.

"I agree, but my hands are tied. I get orders from the board of directors and have no say in the matter." She was clearly bothered.

"Isn't Waldo Dartmoor the head of this committee? I will call him. Thank you, I'll be back tomorrow to have some fun."

Sir Wendel called Mr. Dartmoor who did not argue too much once the name Jake Fischer was mentioned (the head of the London News Station who owed Sir Wendel a big favor). The order to give patients 10 mg melatonin was reduced to 1 mg.

The next day Sir Wendel showed up bright and early to get Rebecca started on her quest for A's.

"I am going to talk to you about a few things today, Rebecca, and I hope for your sake that you will treat everything I say with full consideration. I can work on your memory skills, but you must take good care of your brain. I noticed your lunch yesterday, and I am sure you do not have too many menu choices, but please, no more soda, either sugar-free or otherwise. Try to eat salads, fruit, and good proteins, like fish and chicken."

"I am a vegan!" Rebecca proudly stated.

"That is fine, but the food you ate yesterday was not. There was animal fat in the roll and eggs in the noodles. If you are staying away from dairy, you weren't successful. I think it is fine to be vegan, but focus on lots of vegetables, all colors, and raw if possible. You will need to eat beans or lentils or some other protein source. Your bones will heal a lot faster it you feed them what they need. Here is a book on nutrition; it will tell you how to make a speedy recovery. I brought you a bottle of blue-green algae, which is a tremendous source of vitamins and minerals.

"Next subject, here is an abbreviated list of points from the present political system of the UK and I want you to memorize this. Don't worry, I will show you how and I am pretty sure it will take you about an hour."

"You're kidding, right?" Rebecca was not at all convinced.

"I want you to create in your mind a palace, and I want you to walk through it. Look at the number one in your head. Here is how to picture this: one, I am walking up to the palace and on the door is a big zero and next to it is a small two, the Star of David and a kiwi. This will now remind you that the United Kingdom has no written constitution and the only other countries with this distinction are Israel and New Zealand. Two, you turn right into a den, which is a mess, and on the table is a half of a glass of water. This is to remind you that England's political system is messy and not logical and not fully democratic. Three, you walk up a ramp with a group of people, which shows that change in the government is very gradual and is built on consensus. Four, there is a Swedish flag hanging on the wall with a large number 1,000 across it. This represents that England has not been invaded or occupied for any length of time for 1,000 years. The only other country that can say this is Sweden. Now, without looking, repeat those four points."

Rebecca did it without fault. "Wow that is wonderful. I will have this project finished quickly!"

"Next is the periodic table of elements and I want you to memorize the first 20 of them. Here is how you do it. Take the first letter or two of each one and create a story like, 'How He Lives Beggars Belief…'Hydrogen, helium, lithium, beryllium, and boron. Use your own story and then you know it! And lastly, here is a stack of index cards for you to write your vocabulary for the language that you are learning, which is?"

"French."

"Write the French words on one side and the English translation on the other, then quiz yourself each way every day. I see you have your textbooks here; I think it is time to pick them up again. Now, recall to me the facts that you thought of yesterday for 15 minutes."

Rebecca talked about atoms and molecules and the ionic, covalent, and hydrogen bonds and how they differ.

Sir Wendel pulled out the best surprise of the day (in his opinion) and handed her two large books, *Redwall* and *Mossflower*.

"Brian Jacques is my favorite author, and you will find the most delicious vegan foods in his series. If you are interested, I can let you borrow the recipe book." Sir Wendel looked at his watch and said that he now had to go encourage some of the other patients so said goodbye and promised to come back soon.

"Hello friends," he began. "I am so glad that you are here and alert and ready for a game." The nurses were standing around and two of them seemed especially happy to see him.

"We are going to play a form of Jeopardy today and I am dividing the group in half and the nurses are also divided in half." He motioned for the group to be split down the middle and then he began with the questions.

"How many years has it been since the last major invasion of England?" It took a while, but finally someone on team one had the right answer. Sir Wendel kept score and for two hours he stretched their brains beyond what had been done for quite a while. When it was over team one had gotten the greatest number of points, and he presented them with a very beautiful array of French pastries. The room oohed and aahed and the team scuttled or pushed off in wheelchairs to the lunchroom.

"Do not be too discouraged team two, I brought you a consolation prize." He opened two boxes of highly decorated petit fours. The room clapped and each took two. He took the leftovers to Rebecca and noticed that her lunch had improved. She had a salad, strawberries, and a glass of water.

Sir Wendel opened the box, "I can't guarantee that there is no animal fat in these, do you still want them?"

"You bet!" the teenager responded.

CHAPTER 18

⇔

Finding Treasures

The family was all packed up and ready to go. Sir Wendel had agreed to the backpack idea, so the men wore their luggage on their backs and Ruth carried hers in hand.

The day had finally come.

"Do you have the proposed itinerary, Winston?"

"Yes, and I have the diaries."

The day was bright and sunny, and Ruth's friend was on time to take them to the train station. In two days, they were boarding the ferry in Stockholm for the overnight trip to Tallinn. Then the family took the bus for the last two-hour leg of the trip to Ruth's hometown of Tartu, Estonia.

Ruth's family had congregated in the now closed-up inn and hugs were passed around. The food was abundant, and they were all impressed with Winston.

"You graduate college, boy? What you do now?" asked the grandfather in his faltering English. Before he could respond his uncle grabbed him.

"He is going to be a lawyer, right! And make lots of money!" Before he could answer, his grandmother kissed him on the cheeks and pushed a plate piled with pork, potatoes, and buttered black bread in front of him. Winston had never seen so many exuberantly happy people before.

It was late before everyone returned to their own homes and only Ruth's parents remained. Winston made his way up to the attic room, which was quaint and cozy, but a bit creepy.

"So, what is plan, Wendel?" asked his father-in-law.

"I brought my Russian and German grandparent's diaries with me, and Winston and I plan to travel up to Siberia to have the diaries translated, and then we will come back. On the way back to London we will go through Berlin and do the same thing with my German grandparent's diaries."

The large man bear hugged his son-in-law.

"I take care of you, my son!"

The next day, Ruth and Wendel came down from Ruth's old room and Winston followed close behind wearing his jacket. Winston was telling his father how he was going to take a walk before breakfast. Winston assured his grandmother he would be right back. He just needed to stretch his legs. He walked out and thirty seconds later there was a knock on the door.

"Come in, Serge!" bellowed Grandfather. In walked a wizened, white bearded man using a cane and following him, came a beautiful blonde girl with a big smile and a long blonde braid. Winston also followed them in and mumbled something about forgetting something. It was obvious he was smitten by the young lady.

"This is Serge Yaakov and his daughter Diana. They are our neighbors, and they are from Russia! I talk to him this morning and he agrees to translate your diaries. First, we eat!"

Sir Wendel hadn't expected this twist in the plan, but Winston was thrilled. Diana spoke English well and it was decided that she would help with the translating.

"Dad, we can take turns writing what is translated! This is great!" It was settled, Siberia was no longer on the itinerary.

The next morning Winston was up early and came bounding downstairs looking and smelling great. His parents followed and when Winston insisted on being the first translator, his parents had breakfast and left for the day to tour Ruth's old stomping grounds. Winston set up his computer, got out the diaries, and waited for the Russian father and daughter team to arrive.

"Good morning!" Winston greeted Mr. Yaakov and Diana then led them to the sitting room. He handed the elderly man the first diary, made sure Diana was comfortable, and they began. For four hours the man read, the girl translated, and Winston typed. Most of the time he watched her as she spoke

English with an attractive accent. Blushing, she would avoid his stares. They took a half an hour lunch break at which time Winston's grandma fed them and talked of the large party that they were having on Sunday after church.

"The family is coming, and you are also invited my friends, please say that you will come!" The Russian pair nodded their heads then they went back to work. Winston was exhausted but couldn't let on. He wanted to break for the day, but figured if they could continue, so could he.

Meanwhile, Ruth was giving Sir Wendel the tour of the old town, pointing out the places where she had played as a child, the homes of her friends who had moved away, and the schools where she had attended. They had lunch in a quaint café. They laughed and he watched her come alive with memories. They made a right turn and headed back along another road.

"I want you to see my college, Wendel! The University of Tartu." They walked through the beautiful streets and came upon a massive, colonial style, pure white building.

"Here it is!"

Wendel was stunned, "how many years did you attend?"

"Only one, my parents had saved for years so that I could go. I took the basic subjects and an English class, so I could someday understand your silly proposal!" They laughed.

"But why did you quit? Was it too expensive?"

"No, I had received scholarships, but I realized that my passion was for my family and my community, not as a nurse or teacher, but as a friend and support. I loved working at the inn and serving guests and helping my parents with the daily load. It was what I was created for. Why would I desire to be a career woman when that is not who I am?"

Winston nodded, though he thought about how that mindset did not exist much in the modern world.

"Let's go in and I will show you around!" Ruth was excited. They climbed the front steps, and they were about to open the door when a man rushed out and bumped into Sir Wendel.

"So sorry," he paused, and he and Wendel stared at each other, the kind of stare that works the brain to attach a person's face to a name and to a location.

"James? James Halliday? Is that really you? What are you doing here?" Sir Wendel was surprised.

"Wendel! My good man, I work here. I teach in the political science department."

"No kidding, that is my son Winston's field. He is entering his last year. Do they teach all their classes in English?"

"About half of them. Hey, I am on my way home for lunch. I am teaching a few classes this summer, so my schedule is light, a class in the morning, and one in the afternoon. How about we meet here tomorrow at eleven, I will show you around and we can go to my house for lunch. I'm only a few blocks away in a teacher's apartment house that they provide for us. It is a year-by-year contract which is fine with us."

"Yes, we would love to, right dear?"

Ruth nodded her head, "Of course!"

They parted ways and the couple headed back home. They were quietly engrossed in their own thoughts for several blocks. Sir Wendel was contemplating what nearly every man thinks about at some point during his later years. He was thinking about how wrapped up he had been in his work, that he missed really getting to know his wife, of understanding her and what made her happy.

He rarely took her places unless it was for work, like the college banquets, fundraisers, class plays, and productions. He shook his head. He was enjoying his day and it had nothing to do with solving problems or teaching a class. He enjoyed his wife's company and had never thought in those terms before.

"You are awfully quiet, Wendel."

"Hmm, just thinking about how we should have been having times like these more often. I truly am enjoying today. I'm sorry, Ruth. I am making a change and from now on, you are now my number one mission."

"Am I a mission?"

"The mission is to make you happy," answered Sir Wendel.

"Be very careful, because you may not want to know what would make me happy," warned his wife. That made Wendel ponder even more, would he be ready to make a commitment like that, to do something that he did not want to do to bring his wife enjoyment? The walk came to an end, and they entered the house. Ruth's mother swept her away to engage her in the planning of the large party that was coming up in four days. Wendel sat and listened to the last pages of the second diary. Diana and her father rose, said their goodbyes, and left.

"Whew, Dad, these people are relentless. They never get tired! And by the way, these really aren't diaries, more like journal's that highlight important dates and occurrences. You will be happy to know that your father has been born." Winston laughed.

Wendel snapped out of his deep thoughts and raised his eyebrows.

"Anything else of importance?"

"Yes, I think you will be amazed. We are Jewish! The last name of Salomon is indeed a name from the kingly tribe of Judah. Now you know for sure!"

"So, were they Bolshevik spies?" Wendel was afraid to ask.

"No, Dad, they were honest hard-working people who went hungry and suffered in the cold regions of Siberia. Your grandfather was sent there because of protesting the treatment of Jews under Alexander III. His wife followed him up there and in the meantime millions of Jews fled Russia and went to the United States. Your grandfather never forgave himself for not being able to get him, his wife, and their new baby out of the country with the rest of his family.

"He only spent four years up north before they released him and slowly they made their way down to a warmer climate. Not sure yet how the story ends, but it sounds like the makings of a good book."

Sir Wendel was filling Winston in on their adventures of the day when they were interrupted by the call to dinner.

Winston went right to bed after eating, his grandmother worried that he was sick and made him take a spoonful of cod liver oil.

"No, Grandma, I am beat from staring at the most beautiful girl in the world all day long!"

His grandmother couldn't understand his meaning, which was fine by him. He said his good nights and climbed the wooden stairs.

Wendel stayed up and read the work from the day and corrected typing errors Winston had made. He felt that old feeling of sadness come over him, the one he had only experienced twice in his adult life. He couldn't shake it, and when his wife said goodnight, he was only too happy to follow her up the stairs.

The chipper and highly motivated Winston bounded down the steps the next morning and was ready for the day. His grandmother beamed at his recovery and insisted that it had been the result of the cod liver oil. The Russians arrived and they quickly got going on the work at hand. They nearly made it through the third journal by 10:30, as the process was moving more quickly. With only one journal remaining, Winston was hoping to stretch it out.

"I am sorry Winston, but my father has a need to lie down. Can we come back around one o'clock?"

"Of course, take all the time you need. You both have been such help in fulfilling my father's biggest dream. Thank you both very much!" He walked them to the door then headed for the kitchen.

Wendel overheard the Russian family leave so invited Winston to join him and his mother for a tour of the university campus.

"Wow, Dad, I would love that!"

Dr. James Halliday met them in the foyer and shook Winston's hand.

"So nice to meet you. I hear that we have much in common!" They chatted as Dr. Halliday gave them the grand tour of the now quiet summer hallways. When they walked into the library, Sir Wendel walked off as he was always in a research mode. Ruth followed him and Winston and the professor were alone.

"I wonder if I could transfer here from Oxford for my last year." Winston timidly asked. "My dad may not be too happy about it so don't mention it to him, but I feel like I belong here. What do you think?"

"I think it is a marvelous idea, this is one of the best Universities in the world by reputation. I think you would like it. I have an idea. I could hire you as my assistant so you could finish your classes and do some research and teaching for me, which is a great start to a resume. What do you think?"

"Perfect!" Winston was so excited; he could barely contain himself. Dr. Halliday walked over and pulled a packet from behind a desk.

"Here is the transfer admission packet which you need to work on right away; school starts in two months! Get it done immediately, put me down as a reference, and add a note that I have asked you to be my intern if you are accepted." Winston grabbed the papers and left at nearly a trot.

"Where did he go?" asked Ruth when she returned from the library.

"He was anxious for the future." Dr. James did not want to lie. Winston's mother was thinking of how the blonde girl made her son's eyes twinkle.

"Sir Wendel, I have a proposition for you to think over," began the friend. "The school is in need of a logic professor, and you fit the bill. They also have a call out for Latin tutors. What would you say to taking a year and come and helping us out for a while?"

Sir Wendel, not one for change, cringed. He then looked at his wife and she was grinning and giggling. He had not seen this before. Could this be what it would mean to make his wife happy? Oh dear!

"Here is the paperwork, but if you do decide, you need jump on it quickly as classes begin in two months. Let's go eat."

Wendel stiffly took the papers and was silent the entire trek. Ruth was full of questions and small talk enough for both of them.

Winston arrived at the kitchen table and spent more than an hour filling out the forms. He signed them and mailed them off. He then sent a letter to Oxford requesting that his transcripts be sent to the University of Tartu. There was the familiar knock at the door. The last translation was soon begun. They worked straight for four hours when Diana rose and excused herself. Winston rushed to the old man's side and told him he would like permission to court his daughter. Mr. Yaakov did not understand, but he did guess. The man was gracious and only raised his index finger, which meant wait.

Wendel and Ruth were only blocks from the inn,

"Wendel, have you noticed that your son is in love?"

"With whom? Not that 15-year-old translator!" exclaimed Wendel in a huff.

"She is not 15!" Ruth's voice rose. "You wait right here and don't you move!"

Ruth ran all the way home, then ran back. She was quite out of breath, so it took a minute.

"Nearly 22, her birthday is in a few weeks. I asked my mother."

"Her dad is a sick man, your mom told me. He wouldn't part with her for anything. Ruth, this is a big mistake. Maybe we should leave right away!"

"Where is your faith in God? You had no business winning my heart, but you did, and no one interfered! We are not going back into that house until you have adjusted your attitude! How can you say what God's plan is for your son?"

"You are right my dear. Here is a girl with no tattoos, no studs, or rings, and modest as they get, and I am still not satisfied. You want to move here, don't you?" Wendel was afraid to ask.

"That is why you are upset, isn't it. Pray about it then we will talk." Ruth patted his arm.

The family had much to talk about that night, but they all stayed calm. Wendel agreed to apply for the job and spent the rest of the evening filling out pages of paperwork.

The party on Sunday was a success and after Grandmother communicated to Serge that Winston was transferring to Tartu, he seemed more cheerful. Diana went up to Winston. "Is this true? You are coming here?"

"I've only applied," he responded, "but I would really like to. I have asked your father for permission to court you."

"Court?" she asked.

"You know, I, well, want to win your heart so that one day you will marry me," blushed Winston.

"Oh," she quickly walked away.

The father-son team never did make it to Siberia, but they did find some amazing treasures: new friends, old friends, seeing family again, and possibly a whole new adventure in Tartu, Estonia.

CHAPTER 19

The Interpretation

Iosif, Ilya and baby Pyotr Salomon had walked for weeks with a group of Russian Jews who chose to flee their homes. Millions of Jews left Russia between 1880 and 1920 escaping anti-Semitic persecution. The group they joined up with, had high hopes of crossing into Europe through Finland. While many chose to sail to America, most of the people the Salomons fled with wanted to see if they could meet up with family or friends in Europe. The group would halt, sometimes for a few weeks, to pick up farming jobs along the way. The long summer days were a benefit for the travelers, but it was a miserable and discouraging journey. It included sleeping in barns and in homemade tents along the roadways. The worst of it was the burials of a few older people who had died from the rigors of walking, braving the cold nights, and suffering from the under abundance of food.

They finally crossed over the borders into Scandinavia, and the Finnish people were kind and generous and helped transport them to the western border. It was there that many of them waited out the winter, working and staying with the local people who had sympathy for their plight. When the first warmth of spring arrived, they seemed to scatter in different directions depending on where in Europe they had hoped to begin their new life. Iosif, Ilya and now their two-year-old Pyotr, had the goal of reaching England, where they had been in contact with old friends from Moscow. They arrived at the end of August, just before the first chill of winter set in. Their friends, Robert and Lisa Atland, took them in and for eight years the family worked hard to save up what they needed to prosper in the new world. The Atlands had taken on non-Russian names and more English ones in hopes of blending in. Following their lead, Iosif became Joseph, Ilya changed her name to Leah and Pyotr was Peter. They were skeptical of this new land, not knowing if they would be accepted or not. In Peter's tenth year, his mother passed away and his father soon left to find work in the big city of London. He would send money each week and sometimes a note. Peter did well in school and studied to be an accountant as he was very good with numbers.

On January 15th of Peter's twelfth year a note with money arrived at the Atland's home by a special messenger. The note contained the sad news that Peter's father had died from consumption. The journal entries ended.

Sir Wendel reread the journal notes that had been typed up the previous summer. He was ready now to see what the two German diaries held from his mother's side of the family. He and Ruth were nicely settled in their temporary, but furnished apartment supplied by the University of Tartu in Estonia. It had been a whirlwind move, but finally they locked up their home in London and with trepidation, began the experience of a new beginning. Winston had been accepted for the transfer, was assisting Professor Halliday, and had the goal of earning a master's degree. Ruth was happily back to assisting her parents and neighbors, especially Mr. Yaakov, whose health had declined since they had last seen him. Winston still pursued the blonde Diana, but only on Sundays as his schedule was full and his free time limited. He had decided to live with his grandparents who were conveniently close to the person of his affection and the place of his education.

Sir Wendel became acquainted with the German Professor Schmidt and carefully brought up the subject of his remaining diaries that needed to be translated. The professor gladly agreed to do the work in his spare time. He was a history buff and relished the idea of learning about this family's past.

Some weeks later, Wendel, Ruth, and Winston gathered around the fireplace and Winston read the notes from the German professor.

"Wow, Dad, it's nice that we didn't have to do the translating this time!" He then began to read:

"As a jeweler, Sigfrid Stein was a rather wealthy man who lived outside the city of Frankfurt. He did not act snobbishly, nor did he flaunt the few comforts he enjoyed. He was also a man who watched out for the village. He felt somewhat responsible for its wellbeing. He often gave offerings of food and money to the highly respected rabbi and aided in the support of the few village widows. He was generally a happy man. He was in his mid-thirties, successful and was a good son to his aging parents. His siblings had all moved away to find their fortunes. The one thing missing was that Sigfrid wanted a wife. One day, travelers stopped by his shop, and he was smitten by the oldest daughter, Ada. He invited them over for dinner, and then to spend the night. They were poor and were trying to go to Switzerland to meet up with relatives. The next day Sigfrid watched them disappear down the road but had promised to keep in touch. Summer was uncomfortably warm that year and Sigfrid was especially uncomfortable. The truth was, he had fallen in love. He closed shop and traveled down to Vienna to seek out the family with the beautiful daughter. When he found them, he presented his intentions to the father. It was settled and a wedding was planned.

Four years later Sigfrid and Ida packed up with their four children and closed shop in Germany for the last time. Ida was so homesick for her family that Sigfrid had finally agreed to the move. They left Germany for the mountainous country of

Switzerland. Again, a jewelry shop was opened and they did well for ten years. It was then that tales of the Nazi persecution crept into their little community. There were late night debates where some said they should not give into fear and leave their homes. Many others disagreed. Finally, Sigfrid and Ida again packed up, said their goodbyes, and traveled northwest to Great Britain. Ida's sister had moved there and said they were welcome if they ever needed a place. The family soon put down roots, settled in, and again prospered.

The Bevis Marks Synagogue in London was a gathering place of peace for the Jewish travelers who had made their way to safety under the banner of Great Britain. This is where Sigfrid and Ida's daughter, Suzanne, met the handsome, but lonely Peter Salomon, the Atland's foster son. Five years later, after Peter had begun his career in accounting at one of the largest banks in London, they were married. Five years after that, they had a son and named him Wendel, which means traveler. This is where the story ended.

"Why didn't they keep writing?" asked Winston.

"Nothing happy to write about, the days of war had begun."

"Did you know that they met at the synagogue, Dad?"

"No, like I said, I didn't even know we were Jewish. My guess is that World War II caused some people to hide their roots and their identity. My father had joined the military in 1939 and stayed in until it ended. He was a war hero too. He only lived for four more years, long enough to see me start at Oxford. My mother lived long enough to see me graduate. She would have been proud of my little family."

"Was it how you expected it, Wendel?" Ruth asked.

"A little surprising, but I guess my parents thought the Jewish persecution could begin again, so to keep me safe, kept me from the truth. It is fine although, I am just thinking we need to adopt some new holidays. We will celebrate Hanukkah and Passover from now on."

"Dad, I want you to tell me your story. The one you have never mentioned to me. I want to know what made you a war hero. Why were you knighted? You yearned for years to know your roots and now I want to know mine!"

"You are right, Son. Take notes if you must, but those years are not the most pleasant of times. I had graduated and married. Your mother and I agreed that I should do my bit for my country. The country needed more foot soldiers, and I promised your mother that I would stay in for only four years. You were a baby at that time, and I had hoped that you would not miss having a father during my deployment.

Great Britain had been in one war after another following World War II. Greek factions fought for control after Germany was defeated, so we came in to assure that communism would not be the controller of the Greek government. We did the same for Vietnam, Indonesia, and for Malaya. In Egypt, Kenya, Cyprus, Amman, Muscat, Jordan, Brunei, and Uganda we helped quell mutinies, rebellions, and guerrilla warfare attacks.

Most of these involvements were short ones and successful by the way. Then Marxist rebels battled Omani forces in Dhofar. That was the battleground that I fought in. From 1962 through 1976, our troops fought the rebels until they were finally defeated. There were air and ground troops involved in this war and I was part of the special-forces group because of my degree in Logic. This war is referred to as the Dhofar Rebellion, The War in Dhofar, or the Omani Civil War. It began with a local insurgence, which was joined by communist guerrillas.

"The usual combat tactics had a definite impact on the outcome, but the real success was the result of covert and strategic efforts made by special operations forces and an

147

ingenious counterintelligence campaign. Wars can be won by brawn, but brains with brawn are very effective.

"Are you following, Son?" Winston nodded.

"So, I came up with a plan after seeing what we were up against. There were attacks from within and from without, which made this war a very sticky business. I saw that if we could win over some of the local insurgents from within and move them to our side, it would weaken the enemy. We could, so we gathered Intel from these defectors and learned better how to defeat the rebels.

"This 'Operation Storm', as we called it, had five major points: a dedicated intelligence cell, a team for operations organization, a medical officer with medics, a veterinary program to aid the locals with their livestock, and lastly, a group focused on recruitment of the Dhofar people who would hopefully choose to fight with us for the sultan. The propaganda campaign included dropping pamphlets from the air, hanging posters, and broadcasting radio programs. I remember one poster, which said 'The Hand of God Defeats Communism.' We gave away cheap radios and when the insurgents came in to confiscate them, they also took ones purchased from the locals. That helped turn those local people against the rebellion.

"Because of the necessity for secrecy concerning the plans and positions of the troops, being a war fought among the populace, and not really knowing who the enemy was at times, we shut down all communications coming in and out of the country. It is that one point that I believe put us ahead and led us to victory. The rebels did not have the radios like we did. They were largely in the dark, whereas we had a very organized operation. We did, however need to deal with the cultural differences and that was a handicap at times. The other side, of course, used some of the tactics that we used, such as spies who transported covert information. We finally started leaking false information to groups of nomads passing by and sure enough, the false info was relayed. We did manage to intercept a few of their radio messages, but the Adoo, as the enemy was called, began using couriers to pass messages. This was good because passing notes is a very slow method of communication. One of the final issues was with the locals. There was a conflict between the communist and the Muslim ideas of religion. The Muslim population began to see that communism does not allow for freedom of religion.

"We learned so much from that particular military engagement. The last casualty occurred on May 9, 1979. He was a Kiwi, the officer Donald Nairn.

"I was knighted for helping with the strategic planning of these covert measures and for giving input concerning the confidential international diplomacy that we used. Plus, I helped in deciphering some of the captured enemy radio messages.

"I don't usually talk about it because many gave their lives and all I did was give my brains. They deserve the honors, not   me!"

CHAPTER 20

Scotland Yard

Once a year, the University of Tartu allowed their professors, who were on loan to them from other countries, to take one paid airline trip back to their homeland. During the spring break, Sir Wendel and Ruth, in less than eleven hours, walked into their home again. They went to their favorite spots, Ruth to the kitchen and Wendel to sit and look at his famous Van Gogh. He listened to the messages on his answering machine, took notes, and then suddenly felt exhausted.

Sir Wendel and his wife made lists of whom they needed to contact, Wendel's was extremely long, but a phone call was all that was needed for each. He rang up Donald Wilson, Bradley Scott, Luke Abrams, and Paul who worked at the prison and Roderick Roberts, who had been released from prison for good behavior after only one year. He also rang up Vice-Chancellor Westcott and Brother Thomas. He felt good about how all of his friends were getting on. Ruth spent her days with church activities and chatting with friends.

On the Monday of their final week in London, Ruth began packing things she wanted to bring back to Estonia while Wendel drove to Scotland Yard to see Chief Inspector Newbury. They weren't exactly friends, but he could not pass up an opportunity to see if the inspector needed his deductive skills. He waited only a few minutes before being called into the office.

The inspector shoved a file folder toward Sir Wendel and bellowed, "See if you can figure this one out!" The man was clearly annoyed. Wendel took a seat and slowly began pouring over the case notes, while mumbling to himself.

"Thirty-one-year-old woman, missing for 2 weeks. Hmm, this is interesting, Inspector." The chief was sitting and staring at the amateur detective with his arms folded. He was daring Sir Wendel to solve a case the entire department couldn't.

"So, this says that although a few of her personal items were missing, three single shoes were found without mates?"

"Yes," the grumpy man replied.

"Her family lives in Lithuania and it says her mother is calling quite often."

"Yes," he answered curtly again.

Sir Wendel spent the next thirty minutes going over every picture and every written clue.

"It says that there were no suitcases found but that her watch and rings were all in a drawer. Needles were found in the trash bin in the bathroom. Hairbrush wasn't there but an abundance of cosmetics was. Inspector, may I have a phone book please?" The Chief handed him the large London Yellow Pages. Sir Wendel thumbed through, jotted down a few notes and then closed it up.

"I think I have a lead, have someone call these numbers and ask each location if the lady is there." The inspector relayed the message to an office worker and within minutes they had an answer.

"Sir, she has been in the hospital and is now in rehab for a foot amputation—a result of diabetes."

"Call her mother right away!" growled the chief. "What a royal waste of time, but I am appreciative Sir Wendel. Want another?" The inspector handed Wendel another file. This one was another missing person, a 15-year-old boy, missing for a month, no leads. Again, Sir Wendel studied every fact, every picture and noted a few things.

"Do you think this boy is rather a normal kid with a normal family? What I mean is, he may have run away from home."

"He left everything," interjected the inspector, "it seems that if he was a runner, he would have at least taken his toothbrush!"

"What kid these days does not have electronic games with a console or two, music, or a handheld CD player?" asked Sir Wendel.

The inspector beckoned to a sergeant, "Call Butch's mom, ask her about his games and music."

The sergeant returned, "Yes, sir, he did own all of those items and yes, they are all missing." The inspector came unglued, and it is not worth repeating what he said.

Sir Wendel meekly spoke up, "I have an idea, inspector, I am guessing that he is hiding out at one of four of these listed friends. I would dispatch four teams, three each, one at each exit, and one to search the premises. My guess is that one of those houses has a terrific hiding spot and this boy has decided that he prefers not to attend school."

"Get search warrants Sergeant, and make it happen. I put you in charge! Sir Wendel, here is another one." He plopped a file in Wendel's lap. This file was only two days old, and Sir Wendel again poured over the evidence. A body had been found by the Thames River. The elderly lady had died of drowning, but how did the body mysteriously come out of the water?

It took Wendel more than an hour to study the file, he then requested to see the body. He was escorted to the uncomfortably cold room where bodies are kept in refrigerated cubicles until they were permissioned to be buried. The woman was fully dressed and even though the report said that she appeared to be homeless, Sir Wendel noticed some odd contradictions. Her shoes were a very expensive brand—even he couldn't afford those for his wife. He noticed that her watch didn't look like much, but it was still ticking, which meant waterproof and not cheap either.

"Did she have gold in her teeth?" he asked the coroner.

"Yes, six of them," was the answer.

Sir Wendel thanked the forensic morgue attendant, went back to the inspector's office, and noticed that Chief Newbury hadn't moved from his position of seated with arms crossed and looking cross.

"Well?" he asked a little nicer this time.

"Check to see if there are any missing persons in the counties surrounding the area where her body was found. And Inspector? She was a wealthy woman who had six gold teeth, an expensive watch, and a very expensive pair of shoes. This was not a robbery. This was a murder by someone who did care for her, or they would not have pulled her out the Thames after drowning her. You find a wealthy missing person, find the will, and I guarantee you will find the culprit, probably a son."

With that speech, the Chief Inspector unfolded his arms, shook Sir Wendel's hand, and thanked him.

Sir Wendel looked at his watch.

"I have time for one more Inspector, unless you are all out of mysterious crimes?" This time the inspector kindly handed him a file.

"This one came in early this morning, and it is right up your alley. An office has been completely plundered at Oxford."

"Whose?"

"The philosophy Professor, the name is in the file there. The room is completely roped off, and officers have taken pictures and dusted for fingerprints, but no criminal is going to be that stupid and leave prints!" Wendel quit listening to the inspector, as he was amazed at what he was seeing.

"I'm sorry, Inspector, but this crime has been staged. It is a cover-up to something else that is about to take place. May I use your phone?" The inspector moved from behind his desk and looked rather stunned.

"Hello, is this Professor Dwight Smythe? This is Sir Wendel, and I am helping Scotland Yard with your burglary. Are you giving finals today? Good, you are going to either have to change your final or write another one. May I make a suggestion? They can just write what they know, and everything they learned during this semester. I am pretty sure your tests have been compromised. Yes, I know, but I assure you, if you hand that test out tomorrow, some of your worst students are going to pass with flying colors. No, I would not give them the satisfaction. Yes, you are right, much better idea. I will call you tomorrow to see how it went. You are welcome. Good-bye."

Chief Inspector Newbury sat down hard on a chair, "How in the world did you figure that out!"

"Look closely at these pictures, nothing broken, and nothing stolen. It's a distraction, while a student, or students, carefully placed things around making it look like a burglary, a student picked the lock on the desk and copied the exam answers. Won't they get a big surprise tomorrow! I may go over there just to watch. Not sure though, sir, how you are going to prove which students did this," wondered Sir Wendel.

"Oh, I have my ways. You bet we will be there tomorrow!" With that the two men parted ways. Sir Wendel agreed to receive files at his place in Estonia whenever the inspector needed an extra brain. The inspector pulled an envelope out of his desk and told Sir Wendel to take his wife out for dinner.

That night, they dined at the Shrimp and Dip restaurant and were able to catch up with Jacques at the same time.

He spoiled them with crème brûlée on the house.

Acknowledgements

I would first like to send my deep gratitude to my mother, Barbara Orle, and my granddaughter, Lydia, for their editing skills.

I wrote this book to encourage everyone who chooses the classical method of education.

Bibliography and Notes

Chapter 1

Bijlmakers, Hein. bijlmaker.com

Gruber, Karl. (2015, April 22). Poison Dart Frogs are the most
poisonous animals alive. bbc.com

Chapter 2

French translations:

Bonjour, mon ami- Hello, my friend

Faire- Food

Mon Dieu- My God (not to be used out of context, it was prayer.)

Monsieur- Sir

Propriétaire- Owner

S'il vous plait- If you please

Tout suite- Right Away

translate.google.com.

Chapter 3

Adams, John. John Adams Historical Society.
john-adams-heritage.com

Five Ways (Aquinas). wikipedia.com

Giaconi, Braedon. Quora. (June 28, 2016). quora.com

James 2:8. "You have faith; I have deeds. Show me your faith
without deeds, and I will show you my faith by my deeds."
NIV.

Nance, James B., Wilson, Douglas. (2014). Introductory Logic: The
Fundamentals of Thinking Well. Moscow, Idaho. Canon Press

People and Politics. 25 Greatest Philosophers Who Ever Lived.
list25.com

The editors of Brainz. 10 Philosophers Who Were Mentally
Disturbed. brainz.org

Chapter 4

Matthew 1:5, 6. Lineage of Jesus Christ.

Chapter 6

Oxford University Archives (2007).
bodleian.ox.ac.uk

Chapter 7

Rogers, A.J. Graham. (2017, June 15). John Locke.
britannica.com

Chapter 8

Adapted from Precepts Ministry International.
mcleanbible.com
Burton M.D., Neel. (2016, June 25). These Are the 7 Types of
Love.
psychologytoday.com

Chapter 9

Ambrosino, Brandon. (2014, December 14). The X in Xmas
literally means Christ. Here's the proof. vox.com
Brown, Graeme. (2017, September 15). The UK's most valuable
coins: Have you got any of these in your pocket right now?
birminghammail.co.uk
Tchividjian, Tullian. (2013). One Way Love. Colorado Springs, CO:
David C. Cook.

Chapter 12

2 Chronicles 16:9. "For the eyes of the Lord range throughout the
earth to strengthen those whose hearts are fully committed to
him."

Isaacs, Derek (January 9, 2013). Answers Research Journal. Is
There a Dominion Mandate? answersingenesis.org

Saxton, Dr. Williams S. (2001). Lenin's Tomb. FEA World
Update. (Fall edition). pp. 4, 6

Chapter 14

To translate the last line in this chapter use: en.eprevodilac.com

Chapter 17

Ham, Ken. (2006). The New Answers Book: Over 25 Questions on
Creation/Evolution and the Bible. Green Forest, AR: Master
Books.

Ham, Ken. Ware, A. Charles. (2007). Darwin's Plantation: Evolution's
Racist Roots. Green Forest, AR: Master Books.

Johnson, Phillip E. (1997). Defeating Darwinism by Opening
Minds. Downer's Grove, IL. InterVarsity Press.

Lindsay, Dennis Gordon. (1994). The Dismantling of
Evolutionism's Sacred Cow: Radiometric Dating. Dallas, TX.
Christ for the Nations, Inc.

Physics. (2014). True or False: The Moon Was Touching the Earth 1.2
Billion Years ago. physics.stackexchange.com

Sarfati, Jonathan PH.D., F.M. (2010). The Greatest Hoax on
Earth? Refuting Dawkins on Evolution. Brisbane, Australia.
Creation Ministries International.

Chapter 18

Darlington, Roger. (September 9, 2017). Roger Darlington's World. A Short Guide to the British Political System. rogerdarlington.me.uk

Mnemonic Devices Memory Tools. (2017). rogerdarlington.me.uk

Jacques, Brian. (1987-2011). The Redwall series includes 34 books. redwallabbey.com

Quizlet. (2017). quizlet.com

Chapter 19

University of Tartu. ut.ee

Chapter 20

Forbes, Ethen. Lauer, Suzanne. Koonz, Kathleen. Sweeney, Pam. fitchburgstate.edu

History Guy Media. (2016, November 27). British Wars from 1945 to the Present. historyguy.com

Jewish Virtual Library. jewishvirtuallibrary.com Library of Congress. Immigration. loc.gov

Small Wars Journal. The Secret War: Intelligence and Covert Operations in the Dhofar Rebellion. smallwarsjournal.com

The Sephardi Community. Bevis Marks Synagogue. sephardi.org.uk

Travel to Tartu from London. ut.ee

Made in the USA
Coppell, TX
04 March 2023

13787250R00100